“The moon on my left and the dawn on my right.
My brother, good morning: my sister, good night”

BELLOC

The Coming of Hout

Peter Blair

Illustrations by Trina Schart Hyman

Little, Brown and Company
BOSTON TORONTO

LIBRARY OF CONGRESS CATALOG CARD NO. 69-10652

FIRST AMERICAN EDITION

PRINTED IN THE UNITED STATES OF AMERICA

Contents

The Coming of Hout

CHAPTER ONE

The First Meeting

Dutchman slipped quietly along between the river banks, the black paint of her hull and her heavy lee-boards catching the glint of the sun as its bright light danced upon the waters. Now and again a heron, disturbed in its meditations, rose grumpily from its perch on a half-fallen stake. And once in a while a kingfisher flashed in sudden flight across the bows.

Sandy was in his favourite place, lying full length on the deck with his head over the side, watching the bows cut through the water. Perhaps the movement of boat and water had cast a spell upon him. Why else should he have spoken aloud the first lines of his favourite poem, lines so out of place in the brilliance of the midsummer sun?

> "Slowly, silently, now the moon
> Walks the night in her silver shoon ... "

He paused for a moment, his eye caught by a waterhen moving busily in and out of the reeds, and another voice took up the tale, speaking softly, almost as if it wished not to be heard.

> "This way, and that, she peers, and sees
> Silver fruit upon silver trees."

Sandy sat up, perhaps a little startled, but it was only his sister, Sally, who was sitting behind him on the cabin roof.

They looked at one another for a moment, each with a slight sense of bewilderment.

"Come on, Sally! Rouse that brother of yours! We're almost up to the lock."

At the sound of their father's voice, the two children jumped up and were soon busily helping to manoeuvre *Dutchman* out of the river and through the lock into the lode.

The lode was strangely different from the river. Along the edge was a rich growth of lilies. Sally would watch entranced as the golden brandy-bottles swayed and bobbed beneath the ripples when *Dutchman* passed by. She would think herself a queen reviewing her subjects, and now and again would give them a royal nod to show her pleasure at such respectful behaviour.

Overhead arched an immensity of sky, and on either hand, beyond the low banks, reaching to a horizon that might be two or twenty miles away, lay the flat lands, once waterlogged fen, but now covered with a rich overlay of green and golden crops. To one side, where a distant ridge broke the unending flatness, two church towers and the naked arm of a battered windmill pointed to the sky. To the other side, a keen eye could see a sharp clean-cut edge, grey turning to silvery white, where the sun struck down upon the leaden roof of the great Norman cathedral.

It had been a long day, and once *Dutchman* had been securely moored and supper eaten they were all ready to turn in for an early night – Sally to her bunk in the forepeak, Sandy to his sleeping-bag beneath the awning in the well, and their father and mother to the cabin.

Sandy certainly felt as if he could have slept for a week; and yet it was scarcely midnight when he was suddenly wide awake. Without knowing why, he clambered out of his bag, put on some clothing and slipped quietly ashore.

As he stood for a moment, entranced by the beauty of the night, he became aware of faint voices that seemed to be coming from the other side of the bank. He scrambled quickly to the top, and there below he saw Sally, sitting with her hands clasped round her legs, her chin resting on her knees and her long black hair shining like polished jet in the light of the full moon.

Half hidden in the shadow of the bush another figure could be just discerned. The two were talking together, and Sandy, though not by nature an eavesdropper, sat down on the top of the bank to listen.

"Now let me see, perry merry dixi, how am I getting on? This looks like *Pedicularis sylvatica*. Now what in the name of St Julitta have we got here? Drat it, I believe it's *Eupatorium cannabinum*, and if it is I've been wasting my time again, because I tried it once before, in Cromwell's time if I remember rightly. This looks more promising, but it isn't really out yet. I think it must be *Lysimachia nummularia*. Do you think that might work? By the bones of St Guthlac, it ought to with a name like that. What do you call it, my gentle-eyed Jessica?"

"I call it Creeping Jenny, but my name isn't Jessica."

"What is it, then?"

"Sally. You know, short for Sarah."

"But Sally isn't any shorter than Sarah."

"I know it isn't, but it's just what people say."

"Rule one. Never pay any attention to what people say. You'll be telling me next that Pout is short for hippopotamus.

I say your name is Creeping Jessica. And I'm Pout of Pout Hall, and I'm always right!"

"You conceited old curmudgeon."

"By all the saints of Ely! Straight back to bed you go this very instant, and if you haven't gone by the time I've counted up to ten, I'll jump on to that cabin roof and I'll bounce and I'll bounce and I'll bounce. One ... two ... three ... "

"All right, you old Poutopotamus! You go and bounce, but if you do, do you know what I'll do?"

"Four ... five ... *what* did you call me?? Poutopotamus?? By the blessed Etheldreda herself! This is too much!! And what do you think you can do that will stop me from bouncing on that cabin roof?"

"I'll tell the bishop."

"You ... you raven-haired, lentil-eyed Jessica of a Creeping Jenny, you minx, you witch, you she-child of a warlock!! How came you to think of the one thing that would stop me from jumping on that cabin roof? Explain that to me!"

"Oh, I can't explain things. I just know them. Second sight, like my great-aunt Tryphena."

As Sandy listened to this strange conversation, he found himself puzzled and perhaps a little afraid. Who, or what, was this strange creature who called himself Pout of Pout Hall – a creature who at one moment seemed to be in a blaze of fury, and at another to be crushed by a mere word spoken by Sally? Sally herself seemed not to be afraid of him. What did he look like? As well ask what the wind looks like.

The strength of a hurricane, the gentleness of a western breeze in spring, the anger of a tornado, the kindly warmth of a southerly – all these things were in Pout, as the children were to learn in time. But which way the weathercock was going to swing – that was something that nobody could ever learn.

"Well, well," Pout was saying, "I can see I shall have to watch you, Miss Creeping Jenny."

"I've told you, my name is Sally."

"Prove it."

"You just ask my brother Sandy; he'll tell you."

"Oh, you mean Alexander the Gormless! He won't know. He never knows anything. Now we're for it! *A furore Alexandri, libera nos domine.* And in case you don't know what that means – may the Lord preserve us from the wrath of Alexander!"

Sandy could stand no more. He stood up and was just about to make his way down the bank when he trod on a slippery patch and shot straight to the bottom.

"Have you finished now?" he asked when they had both had to stop laughing for a moment to draw breath. "Because if you have, perhaps one of you would tell me what's going on here."

The only result of his question was to set them both off again. He started clambering up the bank, but had not got very far when a voice called after him.

"Careful, Alexander! You might do it again, and I'm so sore in the ribs now that I don't think I can stand any more this century. Anyway, don't you think you ought to be finding out what your sister's doing talking to me like this in the middle of the night?"

Sandy stopped, turned round, and after pausing for a moment made his way to the bottom of the bank again.

"That's better. You'll be all right, if only you'll remember rule two."

"And what, may I ask, is rule two?"

"The longest way round is the shortest way home. And that is as much as to say that people who aren't in a hurry usually get there quicker in the end. Not that I would think of going to Spalding anyway if I were you."

"I wasn't aware that I'd ever said anything about going to Spalding."

"You didn't, but you might some day."

"And why shouldn't I?"

"Because the beds are like stones, and they break a man's bones."

It was absurd of course, but something about the way he said it made Sandy laugh.

"That's better," said Pout. "At last I've managed to make brother and sister laugh."

"Is that very important?"

"Tremendously. In fact it's the first step and that's usually the most important thing of all. But I'm afraid it's all no use. They did their work too well. I don't suppose you've ever gone on trying for eight hundred years, but when you have and you still don't succeed, it does get just a bit disheartening."

There was a deep sadness in his voice as he spoke. The laughter of a few minutes before had gone as if it had never been, and for a little while the children sat there silently in the moonlight. Two minutes perhaps, or was it two hundred years? Nothing stirred.

There came back into Sandy's mind a memory of a sea-side holiday. He had been scrambling by himself for half the morning up and up across a rocky, heather-covered hill when suddenly he had found himself standing on the edge of a cliff which dropped sheer and straight a thousand feet to the sea below. As he stood there looking out to a far horizon, the thought came into his head that if only he believed it enough, he might have stepped off that cliff into some new and wonderful world beyond.

And here it was again, that strange feeling of standing on the edge of something, that strange mixture of joy and fear – joy at the silent beauty of the moon against the soft blackness of the night, fear at the unknown might and majesty that lay within and beyond it all.

"The fear of the Lord is the beginning of wisdom. So says the Psalmist."

It was Pout's voice that had broken the silence.

"Ah well," he went on after a moment's pause, "heigh-ho, perry merry dixi, and pax vobiscum. No good being down-hearted. At least I've made a beginning and I mean to go on trying even if it takes another eight hundred years before I manage the next step."

And with that he got up and walked away, his head bent towards the ground as though he was looking for something. Every now and again he would stoop to peer closely at what was growing and occasionally he would pick something, only to throw it away again after he had examined it. Sandy noticed that where he had been sitting there were about half a dozen wild flowers laid out in a neat row on the grass.

He turned towards Sally.

"Who is he, and how did you find him?"

"He says his name is Pout and that this place is Pout Hall where he used to live," she answered, "but I can't exactly say how I found him. In fact I don't really know how I got here at all. So far as I remember I just went to sleep in the usual way. I know I dreamt terribly. I can't remember much about it except that I was inside an enormous building, a church I think, or perhaps a cathedral. I was all alone and it was quite dark except for the moon shining through the windows. And then I heard a rather mournful tune and those funny words. You know – perry merry dixi, dominee. The next thing I remember, apart from being rather frightened, is that I was right high up in a sort of tower and I could see the floor simply miles and miles down below. Then suddenly I heard the tune just behind me and a voice said, 'Go on, I promise not to let you hurt yourself.'

"Then something gave me a push from behind, but instead of falling I just floated down and down and down. And then suddenly I bumped up against something and found myself sitting on the river bank just beside *Dutchman*."

"I see, you must have been sleep-walking again. But I still don't see how you found him."

"Well, you see, I realized that I must have been sleep-walking but the funny thing was that although I knew I was awake, I could still hear that tune, so I went towards where it was coming from, and there he was singing it out loud while he was looking at his flowers. What made you come?"

"I woke up suddenly and couldn't get to sleep again. So I got up and came ashore. Then I heard voices and I followed them until I saw you both sitting on the bank. Perhaps when he comes back we could get him to tell us something about himself."

For a few minutes the children sat there without saying anything more, and then they caught sight of Pout making his way slowly back in their direction, still looking anxiously this way and that. He sat down quite close without seeming to realize that the children were there, and began to look at his flowers, taking them up one by one, examining them closely and then, with a sorrowful shake of his head, laying them down beside the others.

"It's no good, I'm afraid," he said, mostly to himself, "I know I've had all these dozens of times before. Time's getting on too," he added, with a glance up at the moon.

"What are you looking for?" Sally asked.

He leapt to his feet and said in a startled voice, as if he had thought himself all alone: "Who's that? Who are you?"

"It's only me. You know, Sally. I'm sorry if I gave you a fright, but you were talking to me a little while ago and I thought you knew I was here."

"Was I? Bless me, now, so I was. How long ago would that be now? Three hundred years or so?"

"Good gracious, no! About five minutes I should think."

"Oh well, five minutes or three hundred years, it's all much the same. And who is that with you?"

"That's my brother Sandy. You called him Alexander the Gormless and I thought it was very unkind of you."

"Tell me now," he said, "and this is very important. Was I just imagining it or did I really make you two laugh just now?"

"Yes, you did," said Sandy. "You made us both laugh about the beds in Spalding."

"And are you quite sure you're brother and sister?"

"Yes, of course we are."

The effect of Sandy's answer was quite astonishing. This sad, stooping, pathetic figure was suddenly transformed. He leapt up, his arms stretched out above his head and his whole face seeming to shine and sparkle in the moonlight. He went bounding up to the top of the bank and then jumped right to the bottom again in one mighty leap that sent him turning head over heels when he landed. He was up again in a flash, now leaping up into the air, now turning somersaults, as though some tremendous force within him, stored up for ages past, had suddenly been released. And all the while he laughed and laughed till it seemed as though the very bells of heaven were ringing out in a wild frenzy of joy.

"So I really have begun to escape at last," he said. "And it's you two, Miss Creeping Jenny and Master Alexander the Gormless, who have begun to set me free. And what's more you're going to go on helping me until I am absolutely free."

He spoke with such force and energy that Sandy began to feel just a little afraid of him, but he wasn't going to show it.

"Now look here," he said, "I don't know who you are or what you are, but I know jolly well that I'm not going to help you to do anything if you keep on calling me Alexander the Gormless."

"Oh yes you are, my boy. No matter what I call you. You can't help yourself now. That's what comes of breaking rule three."

"What on earth are these rules you keep on talking about and who made them anyway?"

"I made them and very good rules they are too, as you'll find out if you live as long as I have – which of course you won't."

"Well what is rule three?"

"Never start something that you can't stop."

"I don't see what that's got to do with me. I haven't started anything."

"Oh yes, you have, you Gormless Gowk. You'll soon see."

"Now then, Poutopotamus," said Sally quietly, "don't you go calling my brother names or you might be sorry."

He rounded on Sally in a sudden burst of rage, his eyes blazing with anger.

"As for you, Miss Creeping Jenny," he said in a tone of fury, "be good enough not to interrupt when I'm talking unless you want to be hurt."

"It's all right, Sandy," she said, "there's nothing to be afraid of. He can't do us any harm really. He knows that quite well himself."

Then she looked at Pout and said to him: "I don't like you calling my brother names and you'd better stop."

"So it's you that's threatening me now, is it? That's a good one! A child to threaten the omnipotent Pout! And a she-child at that! How they would have laughed at that one!"

"Have you forgotten about the bishop?" Sally asked.

The effect of her words was like magic. The blustering, threatening bully vanished in the instant and there once more was the sad, pathetic figure the children had seen wandering disconsolately about looking for wild flowers.

CHAPTER TWO

The Children Learn a Little

No one could say how long they sat there, each thinking his own thoughts, but it was Pout who eventually broke the silence.

"You really mustn't, you know," he said.

It was the first kindly remark that he had addressed to Sandy, and as Sandy turned with a questioning look, he was even smiling.

"You mustn't spend so much time thinking about what other people are thinking about you, because they never are, you know."

Encouraged by his more kindly manner, Sandy asked, "Who are you?"

"Pout," he replied, with a mischievous look.

"Why are you here?"

He answered Sandy's question by asking another.

"Have you a map of these parts?"

"Yes, but it's in *Dutchman*'s cabin and I couldn't get it without waking Mummy and Daddy."

"No matter. Can you remember the names it gives to the fens round here?"

"Yes. There's Wicken Fen and St Edmund's Fen and Adventurer's Fen."

"And what about the little bit where we are, between the two lodes?"

"My map calls it Pout Hall Fen."

"Well, I'm glad to know that they remember that much. And that answers your question."

"I don't see that it does at all. I can't see any hall here."

"When a cat looks at a king what does the cat see?"

"A king, I suppose."

"Does he? What do you think, Sally?" This was the first time that he had called her by that name.

"I hadn't thought about the cat," she answered.

"No, of course you hadn't. People never do."

"You mean that you can see things here that we can't? I believe that you're here because this is your home," she went on.

"Half marks," said Pout. "Great-aunt Tryphena would have done better – if you understand me."

"Not altogether," Sandy answered.

"Never mind. I agree it does take rather a lot of understanding."

And with that he stretched himself out against the bank and appeared to go to sleep. After keeping quiet for a minute or two Sally said in a whisper, "I wonder what he was looking for?"

"*Helleborus viridis*, of course. What else would you expect me to be looking for?"

They were both surprised by his prompt answer.

"No need to be surprised," he went on. "I can hear the wool growing on a sheep's back quite easily. I used to be able to hear the flames crackling on the sun, but I don't get much chance nowadays. The moon's more difficult, though when I'm at my best I can sometimes hear it waxing and waning – rather like an enormous bellows slowly opening and then slowly shutting, an odd wheezing sort of a sound."

"I wish you wouldn't go on using all these Latin words," Sandy said. "What's this *Helleborus* stuff?"

"*Helleborus viridis?* I should ask your sister if I were you."

"Do you know what it is, Sally?"

"Not really, but I should guess that it's a flower of some sort, one of the kind we call Hellebores."

"Well, whatever it is, what do you want it for?" Sandy asked Pout.

"I don't want it," he answered.

"But you said just now you were looking for it."

"I know I did."

"Surely that must mean you want it."

"Not at all. It's dangerous stuff, *Helleborus viridis*, and you need to be careful what you do with it. I don't want it. I need it and that's quite a different thing. Cerberus wants it."

"And who on earth is Cerberus?"

"A dog of course, you Gorm — "

He was about to get cross again, but he managed to check himself and burst out laughing instead.

"I wish you'd be a little more helpful," said Sandy. "You keep on talking in riddles and I really don't know where I am."

"That's easy. You're in Pout Hall Fen – by kind permission of Pout Esquire."

"I know that, but that's not what I meant. Where does Cerberus come in?"

"He doesn't. That's the whole point. He went out long, long ago and he's never come back since."

"Is he the one with three heads?" Sally asked.

"That was even longer ago. They'd got down to two when I first knew him. And then he lost one of those and only had one left. He may have lost that one as well for all I know."

"How did he lose the last one?" Sally asked.

"Oh, that was when the monks couldn't find St Edmund's head. Terribly upset they were and poor old Cerberus couldn't bear it. He was very kind-hearted really. You remember the tale?

"Well," he went on, as Sandy shook his head, "it was the Vikings. They tied poor Edmund to a tree, shot him with arrows and then chopped his head off. The monks found his body, but they couldn't find his head anywhere. They spent weeks looking for it, and in the end Cerberus was so sorry for them that he took off his last head but one and hid it in some brambles. There was tremendous excitement when they found it."

"But weren't they a bit surprised when they found it was a dog's head?"

"So they were! But they were so tired of looking that they took their chance and somehow they managed to make it look a little less like a dog's head before they took it back to the monastery. Anyway the abbot was a bit short-sighted. When they showed it to him, all he said was, 'Poor Edmund, he never did like having his hair cut!' "

"It was very generous of Cerberus anyway," Sandy said.

"Oh, he didn't mind really. You see, with two heads there used to be awful trouble when he only had one bone. I never dared to go anywhere without a bag of pepper in my pocket."

"What on earth did you want pepper for?" Sandy asked.

"To make him sneeze of course. Once he got fighting himself it was all I could do to stop him."

And with that he took a little bag out of one of his pockets and showed it to them.

"But I don't see why you need pepper now if Cerberus only has one head left, especially as you seem to have lost him anyway," Sandy said.

"For my soup. I always find you need a little something to give it a bit of flavour. You see, I don't really like to use them before they are two or three hundred years old, and they sometimes get a bit stale."

"Do you mean to say you make soup out of old bones?"

"Certainly I do!"

"Not – not human bones?"

"Of course, why not? After all I have to live somewhere, and if they shut me up in their cathedral what can they expect? There's precious little else there nowadays, I can tell you. Mind you, it's got a bit easier since 1550 or thereabouts."

"Why? What happened then?"

"Don't you know? That's when the old lot went out and the new lot came in. The new ones never bothered much about bones, but I can tell you I had to be jolly careful about the old lot. I'll never forget the rumpus when they discovered that one of Etheldreda's little finger bones was missing. You see, there are bones and bones and I always used to find that the saintly ones had a little more flavour to them. I knew it was a bit risky taking one of Etheldreda's, but I never thought they would notice such a little one. They did though. And after that they kept such a close watch that I didn't dare to come down for three weeks. I got pretty hungry, I can tell you. Nowadays, of course, nobody seems to mind at all. Ah well, better have just one more look."

And with that he got up and walked away. He was soon lost to sight in the darkness. The moon had been slipping quietly on her way as they talked and over towards the east the blackness of the night sky seemed just a little less black. Midsummer Day was dawning.

CHAPTER THREE

The Morning After

"Come on, wake up!"

Sandy yawned, opened one eye, turned over and began to snuggle down to sleep again, but it was no good. Someone went on shaking him by the shoulder, so he stretched, yawned again and sat up.

"How are you getting on up there?" his father called. "I think I've managed to get this one awake at last, but he keeps telling me to go away and remember rule two."

"You've done better than I have in that case" – it was his mother's voice from the forepeak. "Every time I shake this one all she says is, 'Down, Cerberus, down, or I'll have to get my pepper out.' Very odd. Come on, you old sleepy-head, wake up. It'll be dinner-time before we've had breakfast."

"What's the matter with you? Do for goodness' sake stop jumping up at me like that. Oh, it's you, Mummy, is it? I thought it was Cerberus."

"It may be Cerberus as far as you're concerned, but as

far as I'm concerned it's me. Come on now, wake up and get yourself dressed."

Once seated at the breakfast-table, the two children set to, and for the next half hour they were much too busy to speak, or even to think, except about the next mouthful. Their father and mother sat watching them quietly.

"What's the matter?" asked Sally, when at last she was finished. "Why do you keep on looking at us like that? Something wrong?"

"To judge from your appetites," her mother replied, "I don't think there can be much wrong with you two. I was just a little puzzled about Cerberus, that's all. He's the dog with three heads, isn't he?"

"Oh no," said Sally, "he's only got one left now."

"That's odd," said her father, "he always used to have three. What's happened to the others?"

"Oh, didn't you know? He — "

"Sh! Remember rule three," Sandy interrupted.

"Odd, very odd," said his father, "first it was rule two and now it's rule three. Just what are these rules?"

"Oh, well, er – nothing really," Sandy answered. "It's just some – well some rules we made up, you know. They might come in useful some day."

"An excellent idea I'm sure, and does anybody except you and Sally know what these rules are?"

"Oh, yes!" said Sally. "P — "

Sandy managed to drown the rest of her remark with a loud sneeze.

"And what precisely does rule three say?"

"Well, as a matter of fact," Sandy answered, "rule three is just, well – it's just that you must never speak with your mouth full."

"I see," said his father. "Not a bad rule at all, though personally I always think it's a much better rule never to believe anything anyone tells you, don't you? Well, well, it's time we were clearing up if we don't want to be too late in starting."

There was the washing-up to be done, the cabin to be tidied, the awning to be stowed, the decks to be washed down and a good many other jobs besides, but *Dutchman* was soon looking smart enough to satisfy the most keen-eyed of admirals.

It was a brilliantly fine morning, and standing up on the cabin roof Sandy could easily see the roof of the great cathedral away to the north, shining in the morning sun.

In answer to a call from Sally, who had gone ashore, he jumped off the boat and climbed up the bank to where she was standing.

"What is it?" he asked her.

She made no answer, but instead took hold of his hand and led him down the far side of the bank. At the bottom she stopped and pointed down to her feet. There were about a dozen wild flowers lying there in a neat row.

"So it wasn't just a dream," he said. "But I just can't believe it. I expect it was a tramp or a gypsy."

"He was collecting wild flowers and I'm sure tramps don't do that."

"Oh, I don't know. Some wild flowers are supposed to be good for coughs and things. But what was that special thing he was looking for?"

"I remember the first part of it," Sally answered. "*Helleborus* something or other – something like *Helleborus verderis*. Look, you go and get the flower book and we'll soon find it."

Sandy was back with the book in a moment.

"Here it is. You look it up."

"They're here, among the Buttercups. Let's see, now. It gives Stinking Hellebore – that's *Helleborus foetidus*, but that wasn't it I'm sure. Here it is!" she added excitedly. "*Helleborus viridis*. I'm certain that was it."

"What does it say about it?" Sandy asked.

Sally began to read out aloud.

> "Shorter than Stinking Hellebore, it has a flower like a Christmas rose, and the flowers have the same green colour as the leaves. It grows in woods, usually among Dog's Mercury on chalk or limestone. This plant was much prized by the ancients who believed that it was effective against several kinds of madness, also against cholera and plague. They also believed that it could be used for upsetting witches' spells."

Sally stopped reading and there was such a moment of silence Sandy almost thought that he could hear the grass growing (or was it the wool on a sheep's back?).

It was Sally who broke the silence.

"Witches' spells," she said.

"Dog's Mercury," said Sandy.

"Pout."

"Cerberus."

"You know," said Sally, "I believe it really did happen after all. We can't just have imagined it. There's the flowers lying here, and then there was that tune – perry merry dixi, dominee – I can still hear it as plainly as anything. And do you remember how he laughed?"

"And how angry he got all of a sudden?"

"And how he called you a —"

"All right, there's no need to go on reminding me of that!"

"There's only one way of making sure."

"And what's that?"

"By trying to find him again."

"But we couldn't possibly do that. We don't even know where to begin."

"Oh yes we do."

"Where?"

For answer she took Sandy by the hand again and hauled him up to the top of the bank.

"Over there," Sally answered, pointing to the cathedral. "Don't you remember him saying how he had to live on soup made of old bones because he couldn't find anything else in the cathedral?"

"Yes, that's true, but there are lots of other cathedrals," Sandy said.

"I know that, but ... "

"So there you are." The children started at the sound of their father's voice. "We've been looking for you all over the place. Come on now, it's time we were off."

CHAPTER FOUR

They Make an Acquaintance

Dutchman's engine was running and she was all ready to go. Mooring ropes were quickly taken in, and almost before the children were aboard the ship began to move slowly down the lode towards the lock.

She was soon back in the river, and with a fair breeze coming up from the south, the great brown mainsail was hoisted and the petrol turned off. A moment or two later the engine died with a cough and a splutter – and then not a sound, save a faint ripple from the bows as she slipped silently along, looking every inch the royal ship she was.

Each turn of the winding river brought them a little nearer to the cathedral, and soon it was time to lower sails and mast as they approached the bridges. Despite their late start, the sun was still high in the sky as they made fast to the quay.

"Your mother and I are off to the shops before they shut. We shan't be long."

"Come on," said Sally, as soon as they had gone, "let's start now."

And before Sandy had time to say anything, she had jumped ashore.

"Wait for me," he called after her.

The children crossed the quay and soon found themselves in a little alley, so narrow that there was scarcely room for them to walk side by side. Some of the old houses had recently been pulled down, and there was nothing left but floors and fireplaces, the bricks cracked and blackened and all overgrown with willow-herb. But a little farther on some of them were still standing, and the children passed from bright sunlight into deep shadow as the old walls came crowding in above their heads.

They were greatly tempted to stop and peer through one of the crooked little window-panes, half expecting that the people inside might be as old and bent as the houses in which they lived, but just as their eyes had got used to the shadows they came suddenly out into the harsh, glaring light of a busy street, filled with the smell of fumes from heavy traffic.

They stood there for a moment, partly to get used to the bright light and partly because they were in doubt about which way to turn. Across the street were the remains of an old stone gateway with a glimpse of green grass beyond. Crossing over the road and passing through the gateway, they found themselves in quite another world.

The path on which they stood went winding upwards across a wide expanse of parkland, not a close-cropped city park with bandstands and bowling-greens, but parkland with the grass growing long and rich, and cows standing idly beneath the spreading branches of trees. To the left the ground rose more steeply, seeming almost precipitous after the flat fen, to end in a little rounded hill thickly overgrown with trees and bushes. To the right, spread out in all its majestic length, there lay the great cathedral.

"It's – it's like some stately galleon sailing across the ocean waves, isn't it?" said Sandy – and immediately wished he hadn't.

"Do you mean it looks like a ship?" Sally asked.

"Well – yes. I suppose that's what I did mean."

"But if it's a sailing-ship it ought to have some masts and sails, and it hasn't got either. And if it's a steam-ship it ought to have some funnels. I know. Perhaps you meant an atomic ship."

"Oh, all right then," said Sandy, rather grumpily. "What do you think it looks like?"

"A puffing billy."

"A what?"

"A puffing billy. You know, one of those very old railway engines like the Rocket or whatever it was called, with great high funnels. Wouldn't it be fun if it suddenly started giving out absolutely tremendous chuffs and puffs of white smoke from the very top of the tower! And what a surprise everyone inside would get if it went puffing away across the fens pulling all the old houses along behind it, full of bishops and canons and everybody having tea, and the driver giving great big deep-down hoots on the very bottom note of the organ!"

Sandy laughed in spite of himself.

"Where are you off to?" he called after Sally as she suddenly went running off and began to scramble through the tumble-down iron railings that ran along the farther side of the path. She evidently had not heard him, for she ran a little way across the grass towards an old notice-board from which most of the writing seemed to have faded. She looked at it for a moment and then came back.

"Well, what did it say?"

" 'Keep off the grass'," she replied in a mock-solemn, round-eyed sort of a voice. "Come on, let's go. Do you really want to know what I think it looks like?"

"Yes, what?"

"A cathedral."

And away she went along the path. At the top they reached first a little iron wicket-gate and beyond it another old stone gatehouse with a vaulted roof which looked as if it had given safe homes to many generations of swallows. They passed through it into another noisy street, turning right again towards the western tower of the cathedral which rose clear above with only the circling jackdaws for company. Soon they had reached the porch beneath the tower and, a little timorously, they pushed open the door and went in.

Perhaps it was no more than chance that led the children to go in at a time when there were no other visitors there. The long nave was empty and they seemed to be quite alone, save for the choir and clergy who had not yet finished evensong and whose singing echoed down from the chancel, where, away at an infinite distance, two candles burned with flames of shining gold upon the altar.

They stood there in silence, listening, wondering and perhaps a little afraid. Afraid of what? Afraid perhaps of all the might, majesty, dominion and power? The singing of the choir gave way to the saying of a prayer. For a moment they caught the sound of familiar words – 'that by Thee we being defended from the fear of our enemies ... ' – and then they lost them again in the echoing space that lay around and above. A few moments later the service was over.

The choir and clergy left in slow procession, and it was only then that the children realized that they had not in fact been alone. The sound of shuffling feet reached down the nave to where they stood and they saw that quite a number of people had been attending the service. Just then the door behind them was pushed open and a crowd of people came in, laden with rucksacks and cameras and suchlike, several of them carrying open guide-books.

They had no guide-book themselves, and somehow it did

not seem likely that any guide-book would have helped them to find what they were looking for. As they walked along the nave, Sandy began to think how absurd it all was. They must surely have been dreaming that night in the lode – but then how could they both have had the same dream? Then it must have been a tramp after all, or perhaps there had been someone from another boat that had been lying round the corner.

That was it, of course. What a fool he had been not to think of it before. He remembered now how he had once read in a book about the fens that people used to go out at night and shine torches against white sheets so as to attract the moths. The person who called himself Pout must have been someone like that, out moth-hunting. But then what about the wild flowers all laid out in a row? That need not mean anything either. Perhaps he had been collecting wild flowers earlier in the day and was just waiting till the moon dropped a little lower in the sky before he started moth-hunting. He must have had a good laugh afterwards with all that nonsense about bone soup.

"The whole thing's absurd. It can't possibly be true," Sandy said to himself, though he realized he had spoken aloud.

"That seems to me to be a very profound observation for a young man," a voice replied, "but you must be going to be an architect."

Sandy turned in some astonishment to find himself standing beside a round, bearded man who was not much taller than himself, but who was hung about with binoculars and cameras and satchels, and who seemed to be in danger of tumbling over as he leant backwards to gaze up through gold-rimmed spectacles at the roof over their heads.

"You are entirely right up to a point," he went on. "I agree that it is absurd, but I find myself bound to disagree with the second part of your observation. I assure you that it is true. I know of course, as indeed I ought, that the lantern-tower up above us is one of the most remarkable feats of engineering that you will find anywhere in this country, or perhaps I may say in the whole of Europe. Let them say what they like about splitting atoms and firing rockets to moons, I still say that the man who designed that lantern was as good as any of them. Yes, yes, absurd certainly, but nevertheless entirely true, every single piece of it."

Now as their companion went on talking Sandy realized that Sally and he must have walked the full length of the nave and, while his thoughts were of Pout, he had been standing without realizing it beneath the great central lantern and gazing up at it.

"I beg your pardon, sir, I didn't mean ... "

"Pray do not apologize, sir. I know you did not mean to be in the least irreverent. I am truly amazed that one who seems so young as yourself, sir, should have seen at once, merely by standing and looking at it, what a remarkable piece of work it is. You have a great future before you, sir. It is not often that I have the good fortune to meet with such an intelligent young man. Come, let us walk a little farther."

"But sir ... "

"Say no more, not one word. I insist on the privilege of your company while we go on a little tour together."

Not knowing what to do, Sandy turned towards Sally, but she was not there. He felt a moment of anxiety, but told himself that she must just have slipped round one of the great pillars, not wanting to be taken on a tour of the whole cathedral by the bearded man. Yet he felt uneasy and began to look anxiously about, wondering what to do next.

"I perceive, my boy, you are a little restless. How wonderful! What insight! You feel just as I do that this great nave, for all its splendour, is perhaps just a shade too narrow, a shade too high. And how right you are! But to think that you should have reached the truth so quickly, while I in my humble way have taken years of patient meditation to reach that same conclusion. Come now, let us walk a little into the choir. And what do you think about the reredos?"

Sandy tried hard to escape, but the stranger laid a hand on his shoulder and began steering him along towards the choir. He looked anxiously this way and that to see if he could catch a glimpse of Sally, but she was nowhere to be seen and he began to get very worried because he thought that the cathedral would not remain open much longer. He wondered what might happen to her if she should get locked in and have to spend the night there.

"Nineteenth-century, of course – and quite in keeping with the pulpit and the organ-case. There are many who would sweep away these monuments of the Victorian Age – but not you – I can see at once that you have liberal views – live and let live say I ... "

On and on he went, peering this way and that through his gold-rimmed spectacles, his pointed beard jutting out like a ship's bowsprit, and a hand always on Sandy's shoulder. They had gone perhaps halfway along the choir when he suddenly turned to look down the long nave.

"And here let us feast our eyes ... "

Sandy did not stop to hear what they were to feast their eyes on, but seizing his opportunity he slipped round the end of one of the choir-stalls, thinking that perhaps Sally might have gone there, where she would be able to hide and yet keep them in sight. The voice went droning on and then suddenly stopped.

"Odd! Very odd!" it continued a moment later. "Most extraordinary! Here one minute and gone the next. A genius, a genius of mercury and quicksilver! I must find him again."

Sandy's heart sank, but he thought that if he stooped low he would never be seen. Then to his horror he saw the beard peering round the corner of the choir-stalls.

"Ah, dear boy, there you are! But of course – how foolish of me not to realize – the misericords – of course – wonderful – wonderful – I might have guessed."

And there he was tipping up the old wooden seats to look at the carving underneath.

"Forty-eight of them I believe, or is it perhaps forty-nine? Hercules? Dear me no – how stupid of me – Samson and the Lion, beyond a doubt. And here? The bear and the monkeys – good, I agree, but perhaps not quite so good as the owl and the mouse over on the other side – what strange people they must have been – almost everything here except elephants and mermaids, and I'm sure I've seen even those somewhere. Now tell me, dear boy, what are you looking for?"

"I'm looking for my sister," Sandy replied.

"Your sister now. Let me see. I wonder which one that would be. I don't seem to recall ... Looking for your sister, did you say? Dear me, you must be older than I thought. All these carvings are fourteenth-century, every one of them, and if there is one of your sister here I suppose that would make you about six hundred or so, say six hundred and twelve. A great age to be sure, a very great age! And yet how young you look. I would never have guessed it, indeed I would not. Of course that explains much. You have indeed had more experience of life than I had supposed. And your sister, was she younger or older than you?"

"Younger, sir, but she's ... "

"Oh, she's still alive, is she? I beg your pardon, you said something? No? Odd, I thought I heard you speak, but perhaps my ears were just playing tricks with me. So she is younger, is she? About six hundred and eleven, I suppose. Well, well, what a remarkable pair! And your father and mother, were they perhaps long-lived too? Though no doubt they will have been dead for a long time now."

"Oh no, sir, they're both alive, but ... "

"Good gracious me! How astonishing! It only goes to show how much one still has to learn, and here was I beginning to think in my foolishness that I had unravelled most of the secrets of this world. I must humble myself, I must indeed. Four of you and all over six hundred years old! I would never have believed it possible without the evidence of my own eyes and ears. But there it is, with the best of all possible evidence to prove it. Let me sit down a moment. At the age of seventy-five a discovery like this does come as something of a shock. Forgive me, dear boy, I ... I mean venerable sir, but I fear that the race cannot be as tough as it used to be in your earlier days and I have not the strength to bear the shock of anything quite so unexpected without resting just for a brief moment."

He took out a large coloured pocket-handkerchief and began to mop his brow, sitting down, as he did so, on one of the upturned choir-stalls. Sandy was wondering how he could best explain the mistake, when the stranger stood up again.

"No, I must not yield to passing surprise. I must get back to my study and take up my pen without delay so that the world may not long remain in ignorance of this remarkable thing."

And he gave Sandy a stiff little bow and turned to make his way back down the nave.

"Four of them, and all over six hundred ... "

But Sandy lost the rest of his words as he walked off, a slightly pathetic figure, with his camera, his binoculars and his satchels hanging round him.

"Sandy, how could you tell such frightful whoppers?"

Sandy turned at the sound of the voice to see Sally looking at him over the top of the back row of choir-stalls.

CHAPTER FIVE

Sally Sings in the Park

"All that about being six hundred years old," said Sally. "He'll go round telling everybody now and then they'll all laugh at him, poor old man."

"I never said anything of the sort," Sandy answered indignantly. "I was doing my best to stop him, but it sounded so rude to keep on interrupting him. And anyway where have you been all the time, running off and leaving me alone with him like that?"

"I've been here for quite a long time."

"I thought I heard someone spluttering away behind us."

"Well it was rather funny, I must admit, and perhaps when he gets outside he'll realize that he's made a mistake."

"It's time we were going now anyway, because everyone else seems to have gone and I expect they will be locking the doors soon. I bet you wouldn't like to be shut in here all night."

"I wouldn't mind a bit. In fact I think it would be rather

fun. We might see some of the old monks, and I'm sure they wouldn't do anyone any harm. You never know, they might be able to tell us something about Pout – and that reminds me ... "

"Well I'm jolly well not staying here all night and neither are you."

"I've been exploring."

"I thought you said you'd been hiding behind the choir-stalls."

"So I have, but not all the time."

"What have you been exploring?"

"One lovely place, all bright and shining and with a wonderful ceiling and full of people without any heads."

"Now what do you mean? Have you been seeing ghosts or dreaming more dreams?"

"No ghosts and no dreams, just lots and lots and lots of people without any heads."

"Where is this wonderful place?"

"Come on, I'll show you."

"All right, but we'd better hurry."

They left the choir, and passing beneath the great lantern went into the transept and along a narrow passage which brought them into what was indeed a lovely place – the Lady Chapel.

"But what about all these people without heads?" Sandy asked. "There doesn't seem to be anybody here at all besides ourselves."

"Look," she said, walking a little way along and then turning round to face the wall. And as Sandy looked he saw that all the walls had been covered with little sculptured scenes and figures of saints but wherever he looked he could not find a single one that had not had his head broken off.

"I wonder who did all that?" he said, half to himself.

"Something else too," said Sally. "Come on, this way."

She led the way back out of the Lady Chapel into the

transept and then turned along towards the east end, going along the aisle behind the organ. After they had gone a little way she stopped and pointed.

"There, isn't he nice?"

Sandy looked, but all that he could see was the tomb of some bishop or other and there did not seem to be anything remarkable about it.

"No, not that, stupid – that!" Sally said, pointing to a piece of sculpture that was standing at the foot of the tomb. And as Sandy looked he saw that there was a wonderfully carved figure of a fierce-looking animal that might have been a wolf, with the head of a man lying in between his front paws.

"There you are, you see, I knew this would be the right place to begin looking," said Sally.

"Well now, isn't it a good thing I came along here to have a last look round, just to make sure that nobody had got left behind? Almost got locked in, you have."

The children turned, with some surprise, to see a verger standing behind them.

"A lot of people miss that carving," he went on. "It's the wolf that found the head of St Edmund after the Vikings had chopped it off."

"I know it is," said Sally. "He's lovely, isn't he? But he wasn't really a wolf, you know. People just thought he was and I expect he looked a bit like one because he probably didn't get brushed very often."

"Well I'm sure I don't know about that, miss, but what I do know is that if I don't lock up soon I'll be getting into trouble with the dean, so come along now. If you haven't finished you can come back another day."

The verger showed them out by a different door, but they soon found themselves back at the iron wicket-gate, and after going through it they began to make their way slowly down the path back towards the quay where *Dutchman* was lying.

"I don't see that it means anything at all," Sandy said to Sally. "I know you think that it was a carving of Cerberus, but I expect there's probably some legend about a wolf finding Edmund's head, and it needn't have anything to do with Pout at all. Anyway I don't believe there ever was anybody called Pout. I've been thinking about it and I've decided that it was someone from a boat in the other lode and that he was just playing a joke on us."

Sally made no answer. Instead she began humming a little tune – a familiar tune – with the strange words the children had both heard in the fen the night before.

"Perry merry dixi, dominee."

They had stopped for a moment to look back at the cathedral, and she was sitting on the iron railing beside the path. Again and again she sang it —

"Perry merry dixi, dominee."

"That I should have lived to see this day! I, the Professor, I, Cornelius Candlewick! *Laudate eum in cymbalis benesonantibus!*"

The children both turned in astonishment to see, standing there on the path behind them, the little round man with the pointed beard.

"Forgive me, dear b – I mean, reverend sir – I ought not to have done it, I know, but I was sorely tempted. Yes, I confess it, and I ask your humble pardon. I waited outside the cathedral in the hope that I might perhaps catch another glimpse of you before I retired into the privacy of my study to prepare a learned communication. I did indeed venture to hope that perhaps some day I might have the unbelievable good fortune to see your aged sister, but never in my wildest moments would I have dared to hope for as much as this.

"Six hundred and eleven, did you say? And to see her sitting here just where the ancient vineyard of the monks used to be! And singing in Latin! And that very tune of all other tunes! 'Perry merry dixi, dominee.' Tales are told, I know, that the old tune could sometimes be heard here in the park on stormy nights in winter, but I never believed such idle gossip myself. No, indeed, Cornelius Candlewick is not one who is easily persuaded to believe anything! But now here I am, in broad daylight at midsummer, talking to one who must have sung that tune for hundreds of years past. Oh Candlewick, oh happy, happy Candlewick!"

And with that the little man went skipping away down the path so fast that the children feared he might tumble and go rolling down to the bottom like a ball.

"Well, you're in it now," said Sandy. "Why didn't you say something? If he gets laughed at, it will be your fault just as much as mine now."

But Sally did not answer. She just sat there watching him go. It was only when he had gone from their sight that she turned to Sandy and said, "Don't you realize what's happened?"

"I don't see that anything's happened, except that poor Professor Cornelius Candlewick, as he seems to be called, now thinks he's met two people alive and both over six hundred years old."

"No, no, it isn't that," said Sally impatiently. "Didn't you hear what he said about the tune? About people thinking that they had heard it sometimes, here in the park on stormy winter nights? It must be true about Pout after all. I'm sure he must be somewhere around here, and I'm jolly well not going home until we've found him."

It certainly did seem strange. Professor Candlewick evidently knew the words too, but then Sally had sung them several times and he could easily have heard them if he had been standing close beside them.

"Well we can't do any more hunting now. I'm getting hungry and it must be nearly supper-time, so let's get back to *Dutchman*."

Sally had climbed down from the railings and was leaning

against them with her back to the cathedral, looking up towards the steep tree-covered hill that rose on the other side of the path.

"It's a funny-looking hill, that," she said. "I think it would make rather a good place to hide. Do you think we might go and have a look at it?"

"No," Sandy said firmly, "I don't think so at all. It's nearly a quarter to seven and I'm getting very hungry. Anyway, they'll be wondering where we've got to if we don't turn up soon."

"All right, but I'm coming back after supper and I don't mind what anybody says."

They walked down the path to the gateway at the bottom, along the street which was empty of traffic now, down the narrow alley and so back to the quay where *Dutchman* was lying, with one or two motor-cruisers that had come in since they left.

"Hallo, you two," their father called, "supper's ready. I was just beginning to think I should have to send out a search-party. And what have you been doing with yourselves?" he asked as they climbed aboard.

"Oh, nothing much," Sandy said, "just wandering around."

"And did you find anything interesting?"

"Not really."

"Oh yes we did," said Sally. "We found a lot of people without any heads and Sandy's made a friend."

"Has he indeed? And who might your friend be? One of these people without a head?"

"Oh no, he had a head all right, and he called himself Professor Candlewick."

"And Sandy's been telling him the most frightful whoppers about being six hundred and twelve years old!"

"I haven't been doing anything of the sort. Don't you believe her."

"Well, well, supper's ready now so we'd better get on with it."

After supper the children came out to sit on the cabin roof watching for other boats that might be going by. They had their backs to the quay as they looked out across the river, and for no particular reason Sandy happened to take a look back over his shoulder, and who should he see standing there on the quay but – Professor Candlewick. He was gazing intently at their father, who was quite unaware that he was being watched. And just at that moment their mother called from the cabin.

"What time is it? My watch seems to have stopped."

Their father looked up straight into the face of Professor Candlewick who was so close to the edge of the quay that he was almost leaning over into the well.

"About seven thirty I think," he said, "or maybe seven thirty-five."

Professor Candlewick's mouth opened and shut several times, so that his pointed beard waggled up and down and made him look rather like a billy-goat chewing a particularly tasty nettle, and he positively beamed through his gold-rimmed spectacles.

"Good evening," said the children's father, "a pleasant evening, don't you think? And how are your roses doing? I fancy the grape harvest may be good this year."

The beard waggled up and down still faster and the little round figure began to dance a jig on the quayside. Then he stopped and stood quite still, looking intently at the children's father, who was obviously rather puzzled about it all. He was about to say something when the little man held up his hand to stop him.

"Seven thirty did you say, or maybe seven thirty-five?"

"Yes, that's what I said. I may be wrong, of course. One can't always be sure on holiday."

"Ah, you find that, do you? I must make a note of that at once."

And he pulled out a little notebook from one of his satchels and began to write busily in it. And when he had finished he looked up again.

"Seven hundred and thirty – or perhaps thirty-five! Oh, what a day! Two of them over six hundred and now one of them seven hundred and thirty – or perhaps thirty-five! What a day! What a day! Never did any Candlewick have such a day as this!"

And so saying he danced another little jig, turned about and went skipping away from the quay.

"Well, well," said the children's father, turning to Sandy, "you do make some strange friends."

CHAPTER SIX

Pout Makes Soup

It was another wonderful evening, still and cool now, with every little detail of boats and buildings and trees sharply reflected in the water; and Sandy would have been well content to sit on the deck watching the swallows play or looking at the float of a near-by fisherman.

"When does it get dark?" Sally asked him suddenly.

"I don't know exactly," he replied, "but I should think it's still light till after ten. Why do you want to know anyway?"

"I want to go back and have a look at that hill."

"I don't suppose you'd be allowed to now. Why not wait till tomorrow?"

"Tomorrow might be too late. I expect I'd be allowed to go if you came with me."

"And supposing I don't want to come?"

"Well," answered Sally thoughtfully, "I expect I could work it."

"How do you mean you could work it?"

"Well, supposing I was just to go walking off by myself, then you'd have to come, wouldn't you? I mean you couldn't just let me go off by myself at this time of the day, could you? I might get eaten by a dragon and then you'd get into awful trouble for being a heartless brother who couldn't be bothered to look after his little sister."

Sandy knew his sister well enough to realize that, come what might, she was determined to go back and look at the little tree-covered hill. He got up from his comfortable pile of cushions on the foredeck and went to ask his father if it would be all right for them to go off for a walk.

"Yes, but don't be late getting back," he answered, "and if you think of bringing back any more peculiar friends you might give me some warning this time."

And so they set off once more, and were soon back in the park. The sun was dropping well down now and the park itself lay in the shade, but high up on the great western tower the cathedral still glowed with a warmth that softened the hard outline of the stonework.

They walked on slowly up the winding path and then turned off towards the hill. Suddenly Sally stopped and stared at the tops of the trees that were growing on the hill.

"What's the matter?" Sandy asked.

"Do you see what I see?" was her answer.

Sandy looked but could see nothing unusual.

"Isn't that smoke coming out from the top of the trees?" she asked.

"I believe I can just see something and it does look rather like smoke to me, but if it is, that must mean that there are people up there, so it won't be any use our going any farther. Come on, let's go back to the river. You'll have to come up again tomorrow after all."

Sandy turned to make his way down again.

"Aren't you coming?" he called back to Sally, as she stood there, still gazing at the top of the hill.

"Come here a minute," she called. "There's something odd about that smoke and I can't quite make out what it is."

"It just looks like ordinary smoke to me. I agree it's going up very straight, but that's because there's no wind."

"No, it isn't anything to do with that. I know! It's the colour. Look at it where it's against the green of the trees and see how blue it is. That's why it's so difficult to see it higher up against the blue sky."

"I agree it does look very blue now you mention it, but I don't see what difference that makes."

"Don't you? I do. There's only one sort of fire that makes that sort of smoke – peat."

And as Sandy looked again he began to think she was right.

"Now who," said Sally, "would make a peat fire just there, when there must be lots of dry wood under those trees?"

"Well, I suppose that the only way to find out is to go and have a look," Sandy replied.

There was a wooden fence round the hill where the slope began to get really steep, but it was a sadly battered fence and there were many gaps. They scrambled through and began to climb up to the top, digging their toes into the foot-holds provided by tree roots and hauling on any of the low branches that came within reach.

"You were quite right," said Sandy. "It is peat. I can smell it now."

A moment or so later they found themselves standing beside a tall stone monument, but they did not stop to look at it because their attention was held by something much more interesting. Beyond the monument there was a small patch of open ground, quite flat and almost completely round, and there in the middle of this open space a peat fire was burning. On the fire, supported by one or two bricks, there rested what looked like an old-fashioned iron pan, very black and with a long black handle.

And then both the children suddenly caught their breath as their eyes wandered away from the fire. They had not seen him at first because he was sitting a little to one side. But there could be no doubt who it was, as he sat there singing a cheerful song.

"Sing hokey pokey lack-a-day,
The wind blows hard, we'll grind today."

And as he sang, he picked up something that looked rather like a pudding basin, except that it did not seem to be quite the right shape. Then he picked up something else from the grass, broke it into pieces and, after putting the pieces in a basin, he began stirring them round with something. Every now and again he would give the basin a good shake and then, instead of stirring he would pound away at whatever it was inside, and as he pounded he would sing his song,

"Sing hokey pokey lack-a-day,
The wind blows hard, we'll grind today."

"All right, Sir Alexander, don't tell me. The wind isn't blowing at all. I know that quite well. But then you don't know what it is that I'm grinding in my mortar, do you now?"

At first Sandy thought he must have some companion with him, because he went on stirring and shaking and pounding without ever looking up.

"I wondered how long it would take," he went on a moment later, "and I'm quite ready to wager three pinches of pepper – big pinches too – that it was Lady Creeping Jenny's idea to look here. Wasn't it now? You answer me that."

It was then that the children realized that he must be

talking to them. They looked at one another, neither of them quite knowing what to do next.

"Come on in and sit down," he said. "No need to be shy. Besides, I may need your advice. It's such a long time since I did any cooking by daylight. I suppose you don't have to do your own grinding nowadays, do you?"

"Well – no, at least I don't think so," Sally answered, as the question seemed to be meant for her. "Mummy says I grind my teeth sometimes, but I expect that's something different."

"Good gracious me," said Pout, "how clever you must be! Teeth are the only things I have never managed to grind yet, but it doesn't matter much because they usually sink to the bottom. Now tell me, do you think it looks all right?"

And he turned towards Sally, tipping up the bowl so that she could see what was inside it. He put his hand in and picked up a handful of its contents, letting it fall back through his fingers into the bowl again.

"Well, I don't quite know whether it looks all right or not," Sally answered, "because I'm not sure what it's meant to be."

"Soup powder of course. What else could it be?"

"It looks to me as if it might still have one or two lumps in it."

"Ah, that's just what I was saying – teeth."

And then Sandy suddenly remembered something that Pout had told them that night in the lode.

"You don't mean to say that you're making some of your bone soup?" he asked.

"Certainly I am."

They both looked at him with rather horrified expressions, and somehow it did seem rather horrible to see him grinding up his bones in broad daylight.

"What's the matter?" he asked. "What are you looking at me like that for?"

"Doesn't – doesn't that make you a sort of cannibal?" Sandy asked.

"That all depends on how you look at it," he replied. "Now if I were to chop you up and put you in my cooking-pot, that might be going a bit too far, but these are poor old Irminilda's bones, and she stopped using them a long time before the Normans came, which makes them quite old. So don't you go spoiling my little treat. I've been saving these up for centuries just for this very special occasion, and now you go talking about me being a cannibal. Very unkind of you, that's what I say."

"I'm sure we're very sorry, but why is it such a very special occasion?" Sally asked.

"Just that this is the first time in more than eight hundred years that I've been able to cook a meal out of doors, and let me tell you I'm not going to have it spoilt by nonsense about cannibals."

And he went on pounding away all the harder for a moment or two. Then he got up and poured the contents of his bowl into the black pan, which was about half full of boiling water.

"Now don't tell me I've lost it," he said, looking anxiously round for something that he seemed to have mislaid, "not after saving it up so carefully. Ah! Here it is," he added, picking up off the grass a curiously worked little box that looked as if it was made of silver. He opened the lid and peered inside.

"Not much left," he said, tipping it up, "but still it's a great day and we mustn't forget rule four."

And so saying, he held the little box over the pan and emptied its contents into the boiling water.

"What's rule four?" Sandy asked.

"Don't spoil the soup for a pinch of pepper," he replied, squatting down on his heels and puffing and blowing at the turves until they glowed hotly and made his soup boil briskly – when suddenly there came a voice from the bushes close behind them.

"First I see smoke and now I smell cooking! What vandals have we here that dare to desecrate our ancient Norman castle?"

At the first sound of the voice Pout jumped to his feet and looked quickly about him.

"Keystones and canticles!" he exclaimed. "That was a near one!"

And in a flash he was gone. And from behind them there came a rustling and a muttering and a puffing.

CHAPTER SEVEN

What Happened to Pout's Soup

"Vandals – puff – fires – puff, puff – cooking – puff – tell the dean – inform the bishop – puff – summon the police – fetch the fire brigade."

Sandy began to get up, thinking that it might be wiser to take cover among the bushes over on the far side of the clearing, but Sally stopped him.

"It's all right," she said. "Don't you know who it is?"

And at that moment a familiar figure – short, round, bearded and hung about with binoculars, cameras and satchels – came bumbling into the clearing.

"Ha! Vandals!" he exclaimed. "Caught … "

But at that instant he tripped in a clump of tangled grass and fell flat on his face. He lay there quite still for a moment, winded perhaps by the suddenness of his fall.

"Come on, we'd better help him," Sandy said, "he may have hurt himself."

"Have you – have you hurt yourself?" Sally asked. "Should we go and see if we can find a doctor?"

He made no answer, but raising his head from the ground he twisted it slowly from side to side.

"Neck not broken, I fancy," he said at last.

Then he rolled over on to his back and waved his legs in the air, working them up and down as though he were riding a bicycle.

"Legs still work."

Next, with legs stretched out straight on the ground, he began to move his arms, going through the motions of the breast stroke.

"Arms all right, too," he said, sitting up. "Must be something broken after such a prodigious fall. Ah, I have it! Spectacles broken."

And as they looked they saw that his large gold-rimmed spectacles had broken in two across the bridge and that one piece was hanging down each side of his face.

"Never mind," he said, "always have some spares. Now let me see, which one are they in? This one? No, I fancy not. This one perhaps? No. Ah, here we are."

And he proceeded to remove one of the satchels that were hanging about him, but its strap had got sadly tangled with the straps of his cameras, his binoculars and his other satchels, and he struggled away in vain.

"Can we help?" asked Sally.

"Thank you kindly, thank you kindly," he replied. "Vandals you may be, but at least you seem to be vandals with good manners. I am glad to see such readiness to help those in adversity. I shall not fail to remark upon it when I hand you over to the dean. Now let me see, where shall we begin? This one, I fancy."

And so with much puffing and blowing on the part of Professor Candlewick, they managed to remove one by one the various straps that festooned his neck and shoulders like the ribbons of a maypole, but so great was the tangle that they could only get them off by undoing several of the buckles.

"There now, I think that's all of them," he said, as they laid the last of the satchels down on the grass. "Which one was it that I wanted?"

As he began to run his fingers over them the children suddenly realized that without his spectacles he could not see well enough to recognize them.

"This is it," he said, picking up one of the satchels and undoing its fastening, and as he turned it upside down an astonishing cascade of spectacle-cases of every imaginable size, colour and shape came tumbling out on to the grass.

After making quite sure that there were none left, he knelt down on the grass and began to set them out in tidy rows, taking the spectacles out of their cases and laying them on top. And never was such a remarkable collection seen before. One or two pairs had gold rims, but most of them seemed to have steel rims, and the lenses were of every size and shape from round to oval to square and back again.

Some pairs had side-pieces, but others were made to fasten on to his nose with little spring clips and it was a pair of this kind that he eventually decided to wear. He clipped them rather low down on his nose so that he had to tilt his head backwards in order to be able to see through them at all, and that, of course, made his beard look even more like a ship's bowsprit than ever before. This way and that he looked, first at the pan of boiling water, then at the peat burning beneath it, and then at Sally. His gaze rested on her for a moment and then he turned his head abruptly to Sandy, back to Sally and back to Sandy, with such sudden jerking movements that he jerked the spectacles completely off his nose, and his head seemed to take on the appearance of a clockwork doll.

"Good gracious me," he said, "surely it can't be!"

And with that he began to rummage about again among the spectacles that were still lying in rows on the grass. He picked up several pairs in quick succession, muttering away to himself, "It can't be, it can't be. Or can it? It must be. I believe it is, but it can't be."

At last he chose what seemed to be the biggest pair of gold-rimmed spectacles they had ever seen, and after polishing them carefully with his coloured handkerchief he put them on and looked at the children again.

"Good gracious me," he said again. "It really and truly is! And may I venture to express the hope, miss – that is, madam – I mean to say, your ladyship – that I am not intruding upon some private occasion at which the presence of a stranger, one of a mere seventy-five years of age, would be in any way unwelcome?"

"Not at all," said Sally, not really understanding in the least what he was talking about.

"So kind, so kind," he replied, "but then of course what else could one expect in a lady of your long experience in the ways of the world? And would it be – I fear that perhaps it would, but I cannot get the better of my curiosity – all we Candlewicks have been full of curiosity – would it be a great impertinence if I made so bold as to ask what you might be doing?"

"Cooking," said Sally, going over to the pan and stirring its contents with a curiously shaped ladle that she found lying on the ground beside the fire.

"Ah my dear chi – I mean your reverend ladyship – pray forgive my seeming lack of respect, but, if I may say so, you have preserved the fresh bloom of youth in a quite remarkable way for one of your great age. What a charming domestic scene! Cooking supper for your aged brother, I suppose. Delightful, delightful! And what a delicious smell. A stew, perhaps?"

"No," said Sally, "just soup this evening. Have some."

"B-b-but, good gracious – surely not – I mean – your supper – how generous – greatly tempted – can you spare it? Perhaps just the merest taste."

Looking around the little clearing, Sally saw lying on the grass a wooden bowl with a silver rim round the top. She picked it up, and, carrying it over to the fire, took the pan off and began to ladle some of the soup out of the pan into the bowl. Sandy began to wonder whether this was a very wise thing to be doing, because it was Pout's soup after all and he seemed to think that it was an extra special brew.

"Do you think ... " Sandy began, but he got no further.

"It may be a little hot," Sally interrupted, as she handed the bowl and the ladle to the Professor.

"I say, Sally ... " Sandy began again, but it was no good.

"Some people," she went on, ignoring him entirely, "some people might find it a little too peppery."

And by now it was too late to stop the Professor because he had already begun to taste the soup. He took several sips, smacked his lips and then applied himself to the ladle with such vigour that the bowl was soon empty.

"Delicious," he said, "quite delicious. Never in all my seventy-five years have I tasted anything quite so delicious. But doubtless, madam, you have some ancient medieval recipe that has long been lost to us moderns."

"I'm so glad you like it," said Sally. "Have some more."

"Sally, for goodness' sake be careful," Sandy said.

"Ah dear boy – I mean reverend sir – how kind, how thoughtful! You fear, perhaps, that soup of such surpassing excellence might be a little strong. I must confess that there is about it a certain flavour which I cannot recall having tasted before, but have no fear. We Candlewicks are not easily upset. Yes, a trifle more, if you please."

And Sally dipped the ladle into the pan and filled the bowl a second time, and as she was filling it Professor

Candlewick squatted down on the grass to prepare himself for it.

"I suppose the foundation will be a bone stock?" he asked Sally as she handed bowl and ladle to him.

"Yes, bone stock, and that's really all – except pepper of course."

"Dear me. Nothing but bones! What an excellent butcher you must have. In my humble way I try a little cooking myself and although I have indeed made soup many a time, I am bound to admit that I have never been able to achieve quite such an excellent flavour. Tell me now, do you use your bones fresh from the butcher or should they perhaps be kept for a little while?"

And as he spoke he drank busily away at the soup, ladle after ladle of it.

"Well," said Sally, "I think the bones for this soup have been kept for a little while."

"Have they indeed? I must remember that. And now that you tell me, I fancy that there is a certain flavour of the past in this quite superlative soup. A little more, if you please. I beg your pardon, sir, did you speak?" he said, turning to Sandy.

"N-n-n-no, not me. I think it was just the leaves rustling."

For some time Sandy had been aware of a noise going on behind him among the trees, and as the bowl went back for the third time he heard a sound that can best be described as resembling that made by a very large swarm of exceedingly angry bees. He turned to look back over his shoulder but, although it was not very difficult to guess who was making the noise, he could see nothing.

"Yes, that is it, without a doubt – a flavour of the past – almost as if the bones might be very old – a certain taste of mustiness – of past centuries – of bygone ages. But then I hardly think that butchers would be allowed to keep bones all that long, do you? Thank you, thank you indeed," he added as he received the bowl for the third time.

In no time at all it was quite empty and he passed it back to Sally, who proceeded to fill it once more, but this time there was too little left in the pan for her to be able to use the ladle, so instead she lifted the pan off the fire and poured all that was left into the bowl. As she did so there came from behind them such a frenzy of buzzing that Professor Candlewick jumped to his feet in some alarm.

"Good gracious me, what was that?" he asked, looking at Sandy.

"Oh – er – just an aeroplane, I expect. A jet, probably. They do make a tremendous noise sometimes."

The Professor peered upwards at the little circular patch of sky above, and it so chanced that at that very moment an aeroplane flew across at a height so great as to be itself invisible, though its course was betrayed by a vapour trail which glowed with a golden brilliance in the rays of the setting sun.

"Dear me," he said. "I am glad that the pilot decided to keep high up. Otherwise I greatly fear that we might have been deafened."

And he sat down again to finish the soup. In another moment or two it was all gone, every single drop. He sat there quite still for a little while, saying nothing and his thoughts evidently far away. Now and again his head would nod a little and the children began to think that he was going to drop off to sleep just as he sat, but each time his head nodded there came an angry buzz from the bushes and he would sit up again with a jerk.

"Noisy things, aeroplanes," he said. "Must get the bishop to write to the Prime Minister. Too much vibration. Bad for the digestion. Bad for the western tower."

His remarks seemed not to be addressed to anyone in particular and indeed he was hardly aware of the children's presence. A moment later he got up rather unsteadily and tottered over to his satchels, opening one of them and taking out from it a groundsheet which he stretched out carefully on the grass. He then laid himself flat and straight on his back, arms folded across his chest, pointed beard and pointed boots sticking straight up into the air, and went sound asleep.

The bushes parted and through them peered Pout's face, his teeth bared, his eyes ablaze with anger.

"Shovelling salamanders!" he hissed at the sleeping Professor. "Shekels, sequins and shirtsleeves!"

Hissing and spitting with fury, he came cautiously out from among the bushes into the little clearing, but all his rage seemed to be concentrated on the Professor and he took no notice of the children.

"Spitfires and spatchcocks!" he hissed again as, with stealthy steps, he began to stalk round and round the sleeping figure, stretching out his long fingers as though he wished to seize him by the throat, and stopping every now and then to hiss out some fresh expression of his rage.

"Spritsails and sprockets!"

Round and round he went.

"My soup! My *soup!* MY SOUP!!!"

And as his voice rose to a high-pitched scream, it seemed that he must surely waken Professor Candlewick, but he lay there breathing peacefully and quite unaware of what was happening. It was then that Pout's eye fell upon the spectacles. He paused for a moment and then with bounding fury he jumped into the middle of the pile and stamped and stamped with his feet until there was nothing left but a little heap of twisted metal and broken glass. Every single pair shattered into little pieces – except for one pair alone, the pair that the Professor was wearing, a gold-rimmed pair with lenses so big that they looked like moons.

Pout looked at them and, creeping closer, he stretched out his bony hand as if to snatch them off, but as his hand drew near, the Professor suddenly gave a tremendous snore that shook his whole frame and so surprised Pout that he leapt backwards in a mighty leap that landed him in a tumbled heap among the bushes. He picked himself up, peered out from the leaves, and seeing that the Professor was still sleeping, he began to creep forward once more, but just as he was reaching out to snatch the glasses, there came another snore no less tremendous than the first, and he went scurrying back into the bushes.

"Shirt-studs and shibboleths!" they heard him hissing half to himself. He paused for a moment and then they saw him begin to move round the circle, keeping under cover of the trees, until he reached the point immediately behind the Professor's head, and from there, down on his hands and knees, he began to move slowly out into the centre, stopping the while to make sure that his quarry was still sleeping. His progress was slow and it seemed that an age passed before he was near enough to touch him. He reached out a hand above Professor Candlewick's head and was on the very point of seizing his spectacles when, without the least warning, the Professor suddenly sat up like a jack-in-a-box and stretched out his hands before his face, crying out in a beseeching voice, "No, no, blessed Irminilda, not those, not those!"

Pout had snatched his hand away in the instant, and being directly behind Professor Candlewick he was able to make for the bushes without being seen.

"Stuttering siskins!" he hissed as he went.

The Professor, his eyes now wide open, looked about him as though he was at a loss to know where he was. He took off the gold-rimmed glasses, polished them, put them on again and looked about him once more.

"Strange, very strange," he said. "I see no one but the aged, yet ever youthful, sister and her yet more aged, but no less youthful, brother. And yet I thought there had been another. Have I perhaps been sleeping a little while?"

"Well, as a matter of fact I think you have," Sandy answered, "but not for very long."

"And yet perchance long enough to dream, for if there has indeed been none other here, it surely must be that I dreamt."

"Was it an exciting dream?" asked Sally.

"Indeed it was a strange dream such as I have never dreamed before."

"Do tell us," said Sally excitedly.

"If you were the children that you seem to be, I would not tell you my dream, but since you have both lived so much longer than I, it may be that in your wisdom you will be able to tell me what it means. I dreamt that I was standing quite alone inside the great cathedral at the western end when, from out of the air as it seemed, there came a voice which said, 'Cornelius, what have you done?' I looked all around me but no one could I see, and again the voice came out of the air around and above me. From pillar to pillar it went echoing away into the distance – 'Cornelius – eelius – eelius, what have you done – done – done?' Up to the high roof it echoed. Drawn by some power which I could not resist I walked along the great nave, led as by an unseen hand, and the echoing voice went on before me – 'Cornelius Candlewick – come see what you have done – come see – come see – come see – what you have done – done – done.' On I walked until I reached the door that leads out into the cloister, and as I passed through it, there I beheld the ancient cloister, complete in all its splendour, and not as we see it now with but a fragment left.

"And still the voice went echoing before me, as if round some whispering gallery – 'Cornelius – eelius – eelius – come see – see – see.' On I walked until I reached a door that led out of the cloister, and after going a little way along some passages and through another door, I found myself in what I knew must be the ancient graveyard of the monks, with the old monastic infirmary lying close along one side. As I passed into the cemetery I was surrounded by a great sighing and sobbing which arose from a company of monks and nuns who were gathered there. One among them, dressed in the robes of an abbess, turned towards me and beckoned me, and I knew at once that it was the saintly Etheldreda whom some now call St Audrey. She pointed sternly at me and said, 'O miserable Cornelius! O unhappy race of Candlewicks! Come hither and see what thou hast done!'

"I followed her to where, amid a little group of nuns, I beheld two others supporting a third between them. 'Come, sister Irminilda,' said one of them to the one in the middle, 'let us try again.' Thereupon the middle one of the three, helped by her two supporters, tried valiantly to hop, as though she had but one leg upon which to stand. Twice, thrice and again she hopped, but the effort seemed to exhaust her and she sat down to rest upon a tombstone. 'O aunty dear,' she said, 'I greatly fear that I shall never learn to hop! Reverend mother, can we not just take one more look for my lost leg?' The abbess then pointed an accusing finger at me, saying, 'There is the one who knows where your leg is! Ask him what he has done with it!'

"Suddenly the company of monks and nuns vanished and I was surrounded by a hideous host of grim and gruesome gargoyles that hissed and spat at me, saying the while, 'Steal his spectacles – smash his glasses – steal his glasses – smash his spectacles' – and they took from me my satchel in which I keep my spectacles and one by one they broke them into little pieces until I had none left but the pair I was wearing. Then all the gargoyles fell back as the figure of St Irminilda came towards me with hands outstretched to snatch the last pair from my nose – and then it was that I awoke.

"Well," said the Professor, looking first at Sandy and then at Sally, "that was my dream, and a very strange dream it was. As the gargoyles came towards me to break my spectacles the whole of the air around me was filled with a most evil hissing noise and the blessed St Audrey seemed to be exceedingly angry; but how could I be expected to know what had happened to Irminilda's leg? Did they think that I had eaten it? What have I done to dream such a strange dream? Have I perchance given offence to some of the spirits that I have sometimes thought may linger on from the past around this great cathedral? Out of the great store of wisdom that you and your sister must have accumulated down the ages, pray tell me what it all means?"

The question seemed to be addressed to Sandy, but he hardly knew how to answer it. It would have been easy enough to laugh, but poor Professor Candlewick did seem to be greatly worried by his dream and Sandy did not dare to think what might happen when he discovered that his glasses really had been broken.

"I – er – well – er – Daddy always says it's nonsense about dreams having any meaning at all. I don't think I would worry too much if I were you."

"I am greatly comforted to know that a man so wise as I am sure your father must be should take the same view about dreams as I am generally inclined to take myself; and yet – and yet I confess I feel a little disturbed – a little more disturbed than I am accustomed to be after I have dreamt. And your sister, does she too think that I have no cause for worry?"

"I know exactly what it means," she answered without the least hesitation. "It means that they are in very great danger and you'll have to be jolly careful to see that he doesn't get them. If I were you I would lock them up in a very safe place at night and tie them on very tightly with a piece of string during the daytime."

"Madam, you speak in riddles," the Professor replied, showing signs of even greater alarm and astonishment.

"Tell me I beg you, in simple words, who is it that will get what and what is it that I must lock up at night and secure with string by day?"

"The last pair of course."

"Alas that I must seem so stupid. The last pair of what? My brown boots perhaps?"

"No, not your brown boots."

"My binoculars then?"

"No, not your binoculars."

"Of what then do you speak?"

"Spectacles."

"Spectacles? My last pair of spectacles? My *last* pair of spectacles? Ah, but I perceive that you joke. Ha! Ha! A merry joke, an excellent joke! My last pair of spectacles indeed!"

And with that Professor Candlewick, who had been sitting crosslegged on the grass, tumbled over on his back, his brown boots waving in the air, and began to make peculiar noises which much resembled the grunting and chuffling of several large pigs mingled with the squeals of several little piglets. It was a moment or two before the children realized that these peculiar noises were really the Professor laughing. He continued in this way for some moments and then sat up and, removing his glasses, he began to wipe the tears from his eyes with his coloured handkerchief.

"An excellent jest," he said when at last he had sufficient breath, "an excellent jest! I shall not fail to tell the bishop when I see him. They all laugh at me, I know, for my little weakness, but I assure you that, without counting this notable pair which I am wearing and which I hold the finest gem in my collection, I have seventy-four other pairs. Seventy-four! Just think of that! With these that I wear that makes one for every year of my life. And to think that I should be in danger of losing my last pair. Come, let us count them and then we shall see."

He got up from where he sat and walked a few paces

across the clearing to where he had emptied his spectacle-satchel before he had lain down for his sleep – and his eye fell upon the little heap of twisted metal and broken glass. An expression of the utmost horror spread across his face, and although he opened his mouth several times as if to speak, he seemed quite unable to utter any sound. He stood up and looked at the children through his one remaining pair of spectacles, clutching tightly at the side-pieces with both hands as though he feared that they might try to snatch them from him, and then he began to back slowly away from them towards the surrounding bushes. Suddenly he let out a piercing scream.

"Wizards," he screeched, "wizards and witches! I might have guessed it. Sorcery and black magic!"

And then, without any thought for his cameras, his binoculars and the rest of his satchels, he turned and ran from the clearing as fast as his short legs could carry him. They saw him go crashing through the bushes, still screeching about wizards and witchcraft, and since both his hands were clutching tightly at his glasses, he tripped and fell as soon as he reached the edge of the downward slope. In a moment he seemed to roll into a ball, rather like an overgrown hedgehog, and with ever-increasing speed he went bowling head over heels down the slope.

Feeling some anxiety for his safety, the children moved to the edge of the clearing to follow his course, which by great good fortune took him straight through one of the larger holes in the fence. He shot out like a cannon-ball, to the great alarm of some cows who were grazing near by and who, on seeing this strange sight, galloped away in all directions, tails high in the air. Though the slope gradually became less steep, there seemed to be no slackening of his pace and the children were wondering if he was ever going to stop when their attention was distracted by a positive explosion of laughter behind them.

CHAPTER EIGHT

Pout Remembers

They turned – and there stood Pout, or rather there was Pout propping himself up against a tree, so helpless was he with his own laughter. It was astonishing how quickly he could change his moods. Only a few moments ago, a hissing, spitting figure stalking round the sleeping Professor, he had seemed to be possessed by all the evil and hatred of ten thousand demons, but there he was, tumbling from the tree into a heap on the ground and rolling from side to side in an agony of laughing that made him seem quite incapable of wishing ill to anyone.

"Choristers and king-posts!" he exclaimed, when at last he was able to draw breath. "Was there ever such a wonderful sight? And the dream! What was it he said? 'Did they think I'd eaten it?' Eaten poor old Irminilda's leg! Dear, oh dear! What a lot of fun I must have missed all these years. There's been nothing like it since the cloudburst, and that was many a long year ago. Poor old Corny Candlewick! I can almost forgive him myself, but I doubt if

Irminilda will. Though mind you, I mean to have that last pair of spectacles."

"You mustn't take his very last pair," said Sally, who was perhaps beginning to feel just a little guilty over what she had said about the dream, though he had been bound to find the broken spectacles sooner or later whatever she had said.

"And what was that you were saying about a cloudburst?" she continued, seeking to change the subject.

"Ah, that was a great day, that was. The whole lot got soaked to the skin. It wasn't so very long after the new lot came in and naturally they thought it was some of the old lot playing jokes on them. A lot of witch-hunting went on for quite a while after that, but of course they never discovered how it happened."

"Do tell us about it."

"There's not much to tell really. You see I never had much chance to do a great deal because I could never get properly inside the cathedral and I couldn't escape altogether either, so I just had to make the best of it. There's lots of interesting places up on the roof, and many a long day I've spent up there looking out across the fens in winter and summer alike. What I liked best was watching the thunderstorms. Often on a summer night there would be two or three of them moving round, and sometimes they would all come together in one tremendous storm, and my goodness, that was something. And you should hear the rain up there, hammering on the roof like a hundred thousand drummer-boys beating away as though their lives depended on it. And that was what gave me the idea.

"You see, it's a very big roof and I thought that if somehow I could manage to get all the rain together there would be quite a lot of water. It took me a lot of hard work, I can tell you, and I doubt if I could have managed it at any other time, but people didn't seem to bother so much about what was going on in those days.

"I managed it in the end – a drain or two blocked up here and there, a new bit of channel made out of some lead I managed to get hold of, and then two or three stones loosened. At last I had it all ready with one last stone acting as a kind of plug. Then of course I had to wait until everything was just right.

"There were lots of storms, but I wasn't going to let all that water down without anyone there to see it, so I just waited patiently, and at long last I had my reward – a real drenching cloudburst of a storm right overhead just at the very time they were forming up for some special procession inside. I waited till they got to the right spot – and oh my goodness! You should have seen the flood of water that went down when I took the plug out – right bang on top of them – soaked to the skin, every single one of them!

"I still laugh at it, but it's going back a bit now and they look after the place so carefully now that I never get a chance. Still I'll make up for it all right once I get away."

"Why do you keep talking about getting away and escaping?" asked Sally. "I don't quite understand. You said you'd lived in the cathedral for hundreds of years and yet you can't get properly inside and you can't escape either. How did you get to the river that night and what are you doing on this hill here? Couldn't you explain things a bit?"

"Well, Miss Creeping Jenny, I could and I couldn't, if you understand me. But I don't suppose you'd understand even if I did. You see they were all so sure they'd found out all the answers to everything, and everything would be all right if they just stuck to the truth – at least what they thought was the truth. But it didn't work. However hard they tried, things still went wrong."

"I expect that was just their bad luck," Sandy interrupted.

"Well, well! Out of the mouths of babes and sucklings!! For once you've got it right, or almost."

"You mean," said Sally thoughtfully, "they thought it was you who brought them their bad luck?"

"Good luck too, sometimes. But they couldn't have one without the other."

"So they tried to shut you up inside their cathedral?"

"Soup," Pout replied, after a moment's thought, "that's the really important thing, to know where I'm going to get some more soup from, because I don't mind telling you that I'm feeling decidedly peckish. You wouldn't by any chance have any bones about you, would you?"

"No, I'm afraid I haven't," Sally answered.

"Neither have I," Sandy said, as Pout turned a questioning look at him.

"Ah well, perry merry dixi – it won't be the first time I've gone without supper, though I was looking forward to it rather specially this evening. She was such a nice-looking girl, was Irminilda. I remember her when she was quite young – plump and well fed. In fact rather like you, Mistress Sarah, not at all what you'd expect of a highly respectable saint. I wonder if your bones will make good soup one day."

"Do you never have anything else but soup?" Sally asked.

"No, just soup. Nothing quite like it for the digestion.

"Well, I'm afraid we can't help in that case, unless ... "

"Well, unless what?"

"Unless perhaps this chocolate might do." And as she spoke she took out of her pocket a slab of chocolate and handed it over to Pout, who examined it with great care.

"H'm," he said, uncertainly. "I don't remember having seen any bones quite like this before. What sort of a bone might it be? Nothing to do with rabbits, I hope? I tried rabbits once, but never again. It took me the whole of Lent to get over it."

"No, it's nothing to do with rabbits, or hares."

"Sure? And – er – does it make soup?"

"Well, I don't know exactly, but I don't see why it shouldn't. Of course you'd need to take the wrapping off first."

He proceeded to remove the paper wrapping and a smile spread across his face when he saw the shining silver paper beneath.

"Well, well, silver! I haven't seen bones kept in silver since the old lot went out. This must be a very special relic of some sort."

Slowly and carefully he unwrapped the silver paper and spread it out carefully on the ground beside him, putting a little pebble on it to keep it from blowing away.

"I must say they used to make their silver a little heavier in the old days, but perhaps it's worn a bit thin. And now what have we? Just pass me my pestle and mortar, will you, so that I can grind it up. Sing hokey pokey lack ... "

"This doesn't need grinding," said Sally. "I think all you need to do is to put it in your pot over the fire, and perhaps add a little water."

"Doesn't need grinding? This must be a most unusual sort of bone, but I expect you know best."

Thereupon he took the slab of chocolate and, putting it into the pan, he poured over it a little water out of what looked rather like a leather bottle. Then he knelt down and began to blow the turves until they glowed red again.

"Odd," he said, peering into the pan. "This bone seems to be running away in some strange fashion. Would you say that was all right? And what about a little pepper?"

"Better without, I think," said Sally.

"Just as well 'cause I haven't got any left anyway."

"I think I should give it a stir now if I were you." And Sally handed him his spoon. When he had stirred for a moment or two, he took the spoon out and tasted his chocolate soup.

"Well, well," he said, licking his lips and sniffing at the contents of the pan, "I must say this soup is remarkably good. I expect Cerberus would have liked it. Poor old Cerberus. I wonder where they did put him. I've looked inside every single tomb, and not a trace of him have I been able to find anywhere. But still I'll find him one day, and then there'll be some fine hunting."

As he talked, he kept sipping away at his chocolate soup, rolling it round his tongue as though he wished to taste every drop of it to the full, and when there was no longer enough left in the pan for him to be able to get a spoonful, he took it off the fire and began to scrape up the remains with his finger.

"Do you know," he said when at last there was not so much as a speck left, "I almost begin to think I feel quite kindly to the old Professor. After all, if he hadn't eaten Irminilda's leg I would never have discovered this delicious stuff called chocolate, would I? You haven't any more, I suppose?"

"No, I'm afraid not," Sally answered, "and anyway it might not be wise to eat too much the first time. It might upset you like the rabbit.

"Tell me," she added, "why did you keep Irminilda's bones specially? Was there something particular about them? You said you remembered her quite well. Was that a very long time ago?"

"I suppose you people might think it a long time ago," he answered, arranging the Professor's groundsheet and satchels into a pillow for his head, "but I was never much good at time myself – treacherous sort of stuff I always think – here one minute and gone the next. I know it was quite a long while before Cerberus found St Edmund's head, or at least what they thought was his head. Yes, she was quite a nice girl when she was little, but she got a bit stuck-up later on – always talking about her royal relations in the midlands – never could do with these midlanders myself – Guthlac was another one of them – the song and dance he used to make about all the demons he imagined – and all because he wouldn't stick to good honest soup."

"Wasn't he some sort of a hermit?" Sally asked, as Pout stopped talking for a moment. He had settled himself comfortably now, lying on his back with his hands beneath his head, his legs drawn up, one crossed over the other. He seemed to be in a talkative mood after his unusual meal and the children began to hope that if they didn't interrupt too much, but just asked a question now and again, he might perhaps tell them something more about himself.

"A hermit? Yes, old Guthlac wanted to be a hermit all right, and to give him his due he succeeded pretty well, although the fens were very nearly too much for him. Of course they were very different in those days – water almost everywhere, especially in winter-time, and it was very easy to get a nasty go of the miasmic megrims unless you took good care of yourself. Not that I was much troubled that way myself. Too many jellied eels, that was Guthlac's undoing. He gave them up in the end and stuck to lampreys and then things were much better."

"I don't see why you wanted Irminilda's bones specially, if you don't like midlanders," Sally said.

"Well, come to think of it, I daresay she wouldn't have made better soup than the general run of saints. It wasn't that so much. She always reminded me of one of the greatest triumphs in the life of Pout, and if I hadn't had it all to think about I don't know how I should have managed to keep going all these years. Let me see now – it was on the night of the twelfth of February – I remember that quite well – and it would be – er – yes – six hundred and thirty-seven years ago last February. In fact this is really the year 637 P.P.T."

"What on earth does that mean?" Sandy asked.

"*Post Pouti Triumphum* of course! What else could it possibly mean? Now don't keep interrupting. You don't mean to tell me you don't understand what *Post Pouti Triumphum* means? Oh well, I'm not going to tell you. You'll just have to work it out for yourselves. They thought they'd got me properly tamed and to give them all credit I must admit that their stuff was pretty strong. They believed in it anyway and if you believe something enough – well, I expect you'll find out one day what happens as a result – but it wasn't quite strong enough, and I still had just that much freedom. I don't know whether their stuff would still be as strong today, mind you. Personally I rather doubt it, but then I haven't been very far afield lately and I've only hearsay to go by."

Whether he was doing it deliberately or not the children couldn't tell, but, having roused their curiosity, his rambling talk suddenly stopped, and there was a moment's silence as they both wondered whether it would be best to prod him with another question or to keep quiet and wait patiently. After a moment or two he went on again.

"Thought I'd gone to sleep, didn't you? – and couldn't quite decide whether to give me a prod, could you? Well take my advice, never prod Pout. Yes – that was it, the year 637 after Pout's triumph."

"That's what *Post Pouti Triumphum* means," Sandy whispered to Sally, forgetting for the moment how sharp Pout's hearing was, and fearing, as soon as he had spoken, that his interruption might have put him in a bad temper again; but all was well.

"Altogether it took me about five years' work, but I suppose that wasn't so bad when you think that I was absolutely single-handed, though I must admit that I had a little help from the lightning. In fact I think that must have been what gave me the idea in the first place. You'd be surprised how often the lightning does strike up there. In those days they didn't have any lightning conductors like they do now. My first idea was to start taking it down stone by stone from the top, but after I'd got a few stones loose I could see that that wasn't going to work at all. Certainly it was rather fun giving them the last push, but they soon began to realize that something was going on and they kept sending stone-masons up to do repairs. I suppose you know what I'm talking about?" he suddenly asked.

"About the cathedral, I think," Sandy answered, "but I'm not sure what part of it."

"The old tower," Pout replied. "There used to be a huge one in the middle before old Alan built his lantern that the Professor thinks is so wonderful. I agree it's not bad, but you should have seen the old tower the Normans put up first. Right in the centre it was, and wonderful work. I suppose it was that that made me all the more determined to succeed, just to show them I was more than a match for any Normans. Well, after I'd given up the idea of taking it down stone by stone, I sat down and thought for a few years, and then I suddenly realized that I'd been breaking rule five, and of course as long as I was doing that there wasn't a hope of success."

"What's rule five?" asked Sally. "You've told us about the first four, but I don't think you've ever mentioned rule five."

"Have I not? I always think it's one of the most important of the lot. 'Never do anything yourself if you can persuade anyone else to do it for you.' "

"Isn't that rather a selfish rule? I don't think Mummy and Daddy would agree with that rule if we tried to keep to it."

"No, I don't suppose they would, and not many other people would either, but that's because they haven't thought about it enough. You try sitting up on the roof night after night for years on end, just watching the stars and with no one to talk to, then you'll learn a thing or two – and on the whole I advise you to wear boots while you're doing it, good heavy ones. They stop you from taking too many flights of fancy, and flights of fancy can be dangerous things, especially when you're sitting on a roof. Even old Corny knows that. Next time you meet him, you just ask him why he always wears brown boots."

"I don't quite see how you could avoid breaking rule five anyway if you were sitting up there all alone."

"Well that, my gormless boy, only goes to show what a lot you've still got to learn. People often make the mistake of thinking they're alone when there's nobody there, but not Pout Esquire. He's much too clever for that. There may not have been any people, at least not exactly what you would call people, but there were certainly things, and plenty of them."

"What sort of things?"

"Gargoyles – and things like gargoyles, but it wasn't always easy to tell one from t'other. The trouble with you people nowadays is that you all walk about with your eyes on the ground and never look up. I know that because I never see anything but the tops of people's heads when I look down. You'd be surprised what a lot you can get a gargoyle to do for you if you set about it the right way. Of course you need to choose the right one for the right job, otherwise there may be trouble.

"You don't imagine the chaps who made them thought they were just going to sit there doing nothing, do you? Oh dear me no! They've all got jobs to do. My real difficulty was to find one with a grudge against things. You know what I mean – the sort that would really put his mind to doing a bit of damage.

"It took me quite a long while, but I found one in the end, a real beauty, with great big popping eyes and ears just like a donkey. He had his fingers in the corners of his mouth stretching it wide open so that the water could come running out when it rained. And his teeth – my goodness, you should have seen his teeth – great jagged zigzag things they were. And it was the teeth that did the trick. You see, the mason that carved him got just a little bit careless and his chisel slipped and knocked the end off one of those teeth – one of the very front ones too – and you can guess what that meant."

"What?" the children both asked at the same time.

"Toothache, of course! Nagging, stabbing toothache, bad enough in the summer but agonizing in the winter when the rain-drops froze on it. Year after year it went on and there was absolutely nothing he could do about it. Can you wonder that the poor chap was gradually filled with a most terrible hatred towards all stone-masons and their works? My goodness, how he burned with hatred. I had to move very carefully at first in case he mistook me for a stone-mason, not that I would have been in any real danger so long as I kept my head. They're powerful creatures, gargoyles, but they've no brains at all, and that's what counts in the end. You're safe enough once you learn how to handle people without any brains.

"Well, once I'd discovered him I took great care not to hurry him too much – just a word or two now and again – a sympathetic inquiry about the toothache on a warm spring day when I guessed it wouldn't be too bad. That worked wonders, but I was careful to keep out of his way when the wind was in the east. You see, my first job was to persuade him to move, and that wasn't easy. On the whole gargoyles are remarkably home-loving creatures and they almost always insist on staying where they're put in the first place. Old Loppy Lugs – that's what I used to call him, because of his ears, you know – he was no exception in spite of the toothache, and I must admit that he had a very nice situation, high up on the western tower with an open view, no chance of getting built up and a good long drop for the water. He found the jackdaws a bit tiresome, but they soon learned to keep clear of him on his worst days.

"I began with a little flattery, telling him what a handsome chap he was and all the rest of it, and then little by little I began to suggest to him that if I were him, I wasn't sure that I would like to go on living there always – the neighbours, you know – very nice people of course and nothing that you could pick on exactly, but – well – there had been a little talk – people were saying that the western tower was going down a bit – and so terribly hot in the summer looking straight at the sun like that – he hadn't heard that the people on the central tower rather looked down on them? How surprising – thought that was common knowledge.

"And so on – fairly crude stuff I know, but it prepared the ground and it did loosen him just that little bit in his bed. Then I moved on to talk about stone-masons – what careless people they are – and as for the chap that had broken his tooth, well boiling oil was much too good for him – what a pity he'd been dead for so long and that we couldn't get at him.

"I let that sink in for a bit and then when I thought the time was ripe, I began to suggest that even if the stonemason was beyond our reach, we could still get our revenge on him. How? By destroying some of his other work. And at that Loppy Lugs fairly began to rattle about in his socket. Now was the time to strike I thought, so I said that any gargoyle of even reasonable standing ought not to have any difficulty with such a simple little job, but so far, although I'd searched the place from end to end, I hadn't been able to find a single one that really looked up to it. And that did the trick. He came clean away from his socket and I knew that I'd won the first part of the battle.

"Then it was simply a matter of rain and frost, or very

nearly so. Once I'd persuaded him to move it was easy enough to get him to go to the particular place where I wanted him, a very nice place in a good neighbourhood up above one of the great arches that supported the central tower. He was a bit disgruntled at first when he found that he didn't catch nearly so much rainwater to spit out of his mouth, but I told him that it was rather common to spit out a lot of water and that nowadays all the best gargoyles just let it out in little drops.

"You see, I didn't want a great flood. They'd have discovered that something was wrong while there was still time to put it right and I certainly didn't want that to happen."

There was another pause, and this time it lasted so long that the children began to wonder if he was going to tell them any more, but they sat there quietly, remembering what he had told them about prodding. And then he went on again.

"Little drops of water, that's all. Then a good hard frost. Each time the water froze, the crack split a little wider, and the next time the water went in a little deeper. So it went on winter after winter. Poor old Loppy Lugs, how his tooth ached. I hadn't told him at first that his new home was to be round on the east side of the central tower and of course on that side he got the full blast of the east winds that came scorching across the fens all the way from Siberia. He suffered the most terrible agonies of toothache and I expect he often longed for his nice warm bed on the west side of the other tower, but of course he never said so. I kept telling him what nice people his new neighbours were and how much higher he had risen in the world.

"On and on it went. Slowly but surely the crack spread downwards. At first you could hardly see it, but it needed only a winter or two till you could get a finger into it. Loppy Lugs kept on dripping just where I wanted him to. Now and again I would give a little help by picking out a little mortar, but mostly I just left it all to Loppy Lugs and the frost, just going along occasionally to see how things were getting on. I didn't want to go there too often in case the people down below should begin to get suspicious, but they never discovered, at least not until it was too late. I remember what a tremendous to-do there was when at last they did discover, but by that time the crack had spread right down to the top of the arch that was carrying the weight."

"Why didn't they find out sooner?" Sandy asked, adding hastily in case he had given him offence, "How clever you must have been about it all."

"Well, I suppose it was mainly due to my own cleverness, though I must admit that it was a lot darker inside then. None of this electricity they have nowadays, just candles, and the monks never thought much of wandering about in the towers with only candles to show them the way, so they mostly left that sort of thing till the summer.

"It was an unusually bright autumn day that finally gave the show away. They had the west doors open and the light was thrown up from the floor towards the roof. I happened to be looking into the nave at the time – there's a little window high up under the roof and you can see right along the nave from there. I saw a little group of them standing beneath the tower and pointing upwards. Then one of them went running off and came back a few moments later with a whole lot more. Even the abbot himself was there, and what a hubbub there was! It was just like looking down on an ant's nest, with everyone scurrying about this way and that and no one knowing what to do next. After a little while about a dozen of the bolder ones climbed up the tower to have a look and then they found out just how far things had really gone. I was up there myself a few nights later in a strongish wind and I can tell you I was pretty scared when I felt the tower beginning to sway underneath me, and as for poor old Loppy Lugs, he looked as if he might be seasick any minute.

"Of course they had to give up using that part of the cathedral altogether because they knew it wasn't safe, and they held most of their services in St Catherine's chapel, which was far enough away to be reasonably secure. Christmas passed while they were still wondering what to do. It was much too big a job for them to start taking the whole tower down and anyway it would have been risky having a lot of men working on it. A heavy snowstorm might have brought the whole thing crashing down, but there wasn't any snow that winter – just rain. Day after day and week after week it went on with the rain-clouds driving in from the south-west; and Loppy Lugs went on dripping and dripping away into the crack.

"I had a feeling we were getting near the end now, so early in February I made one or two slight changes in the run of the water so that instead of just dripping it came running out fairly fast, right down the full length of the crack, and even spilling down on to the floor of the nave below when the weather was very wet. But still it held and I began to wonder if I was going to succeed after all. Then suddenly one night the wind changed. It swung clean round to the east and blew away all the rain-clouds. I remember it was the night of the tenth of February and the next day dawned bright and clear – an astonishing sight, with mile upon mile of water wherever you looked. There was no getting away from the isle then, unless you had a boat, but for all the bright sun there was a bite in the wind that stirred up the toothache in poor old Loppy Lugs. And then when night came, with the stars dancing in the flood water, the frost came too, hard, keen and silent. Down and down went the temperature, and even with the dawning of the next day still it went down. The little pools that had collected here and there on the roof were soon frozen solid and the frost crept deep into that great crack where the stones had soaked up the water like sponges.

"That evening, the twelfth of February, they had all been to Irminilda's shrine – I fancy it may have been her birthday or something of that sort – and they were making their way back in procession to St Catherine's chapel, keeping as far away from underneath the tower as they could, when the first stone fell with a crash, shattering into fragments as it hit the floor beneath the tower arch. I knew it couldn't be long now and so did the monks. They were off as fast as they could go. But nothing more happened for an hour or two. I'd gone off to the western tower myself, for I thought it would be as safe a place as any. The night was as still as the grave, but every now and again the silence would be broken with a crack like a whip-lash that started all the jackdaws from their roosts – and then, as I was getting frozen stiff myself with the bitter cold, suddenly I saw that whole gigantic tower, jet black against the starlit sky, begin to tilt slowly away from me. For a moment it seemed to hang like a breaking wave and then down it went with a cataclysmic roar that shook the very firmament of heaven itself."

CHAPTER NINE

Sally Manages Things

"So that's what you call your triumph," Sandy said at last. "I don't think that's much to boast about. It reminds me of a summer holiday we had once by the sea. I'd built a marvellous sand-castle and some horrid great fat man came tramping along without looking where he was going and knocked it all down. You've done just what the fat man did to my sand-castle."

"And just what the tide would have done in any case an hour or two later."

"Yes, but that's different. The tide wouldn't have knocked the tower down like you did."

"I didn't knock it down."

"What an awful liar you are," Sandy replied rather angrily. "First you tell us a long story about how you knocked the tower down and then you say you didn't knock it down."

"And no more I did, as you'd realize if you'd been listening properly. It was the rain and the frost, and mind you, the monks were a bit to blame too. After all it was their cathedral and there wasn't much I could have done if they'd kept their eyes open."

"Well, you can't say you didn't move Loppy Lugs, can you?"

"Oh yes I could, quite easily, if I wanted to, and how would you know whether I did or not anyway as you seem to think I'm such a liar?"

"What happened to poor Loppy Lugs?" Sally asked. "I felt terribly sorry for him with all that toothache. I must say I think it was rather mean of you to go and use him like that. After all, he didn't know what he was doing."

"I know he didn't but you needn't suppose, my dear, that there's anything unusual in that. After all, you and your angry brother don't know what you're doing either. You may think that you do, but I can assure you that you don't. If you did you'd think two or three times before doing it, but even that wouldn't be any good, because you'd probably still want to go on with it. But you can set your mind at rest about Loppy Lugs. He's as happy as a sandboy. He did have rather a nasty tumble but he ended up more or less on top of the pile and in the fall all his teeth were knocked clean out, so he's never had any more toothache, and he's gone back to his nice comfortable bed on the western tower where the sun keeps him warm as he gets older."

"You know," said Sally, after another short silence, "you still haven't told us much."

"I've told you all about the tower. What more do you want to know?"

"That's not what I meant. You haven't told us who you are."

"Yes I have. I'm Pout Esquire of Pout Hall Fen. I told you that the other night."

"Yes, but what were you doing there?"

"Dear oh dear, what short memories people have. Didn't I tell you I was looking for *Helleborus viridis*?"

"Yes, I know you told us that. Do you often go to Pout Hall Fen?"

"That depends on what you mean by often. As a matter of fact I can't manage more than once a century at the moment so the other night's visit was the sixth P.P.T."

"Do you mean to say that we just happened to be there on the one night in a whole hundred years when it was possible to find you?" Sandy asked.

"Yes, I mean just that. They wouldn't let me go more often, and that's why it's all taking rather a long time. I owe even that much to Cerberus, really. They were so pleased with him at finding St Edmund's head that they left me just that much freedom. It's finding Cerberus that's going to be the real trouble. You see, I don't know what they did with him, and I'm relying a good deal on *Helleborus viridis*. It's the best stuff I know, but I don't seem able to find it."

"I don't think you will, either," said Sally quietly.

"And why not, Mistress Sarah?"

"Because it doesn't grow in the fens."

"Golly, look at the time!" Sandy said. "We must be off or we'll have Mummy and Daddy getting the police out to look for us."

It was long past ten and the light was beginning to fade, especially within the little clump of trees where they were sitting.

"Come on, Sally, hurry up or I jolly well won't come on any more walks with you."

"All right, I'm coming, but what are we going to do with Professor Candlewick's things?"

"Perhaps we'd better take them with us, but for goodness' sake hurry up."

"Hey, wait a minute, wait a minute!" Pout broke in.

"You can't just go off like this. How on earth am I going to find my flower if it doesn't grow in the fens and I can't get anywhere else except the fens? Here! Wait! Hi!"

But meanwhile the children had gathered up the Professor's belongings, all except the broken glasses, and were making their way as quickly as they could down the hill.

They were soon out of the park and had just turned into the narrow alley between the old houses when they both stopped, suddenly realizing that they could not very well take all the Professor's things back to *Dutchman*.

Just as they were wondering what to do Sandy's eye was caught by a movement inside the room that lay beyond one of the crooked little windows overlooking the alley. There seemed to be something familiar about the figure, and, signalling to Sally to keep quiet, he crept a little closer so that he could get a better view. As Sandy watched, someone inside lit an oil lamp and by its light a very remarkable sight was revealed.

Except for the space occupied by the fireplace, all the walls that Sandy could see were lined from floor to ceiling with books, not neatly arranged on shelves as books usually are, but lying in a state of almost unimaginable confusion. Some, but only very few, stood upright on the shelves, while others lay on their sides or on their backs. Some were open, some were closed and some were full of little slips of paper marking particular pages. And it was not only the walls. Books lay in even greater confusion on the floor, sometimes in great piles that leant over at perilous angles. Upon the topmost book of one of the higher piles, swaying gently from side to side but never quite overbalancing, there sat a large ginger cat, seemingly rocking himself to sleep.

The table too -- that was covered with books, most of them lying open and in such big piles that the topmost could only have been reached by climbing up on a chair. The only space that seemed to be clear of books was a narrow and crooked passage which led between disorderly walls of books from the door to an old-fashioned, high-backed rocking chair – and there on the chair – yes, there could be no mistake about it – there was the figure of Professor Candlewick. He was rocking himself backwards and forwards, but in a rather agitated way, and every now and again he would stop with a jerk and look anxiously round the room, though never, fortunately, directly at the window, at which by this time he might have seen Sally's face as well as Sandy's.

They both watched, ready to duck out of sight in an instant. A moment afterwards the Professor got up from his chair and made his way with some difficulty to his table, upon which there was, lying on top of one of the open books, a large ball of very thick string; but all the time he was holding tightly with both hands to his gold-rimmed spectacles, his one remaining pair. For a moment, after looking carefully round the room, he would let go with one hand, holding all the tighter with the other, and with his free hand he would take hold of the end of the ball of string and try, for some reason which at first they did not properly understand, to get the end of the string behind his head. It was Sally who first realized what he was trying to do.

"Don't you see?" she whispered. "He's trying to tie them on with string the way I told him to, but he daren't let go with both hands at once. Poor old Professor, we'd better go in and help him."

"But we can't possibly do that. He thought that we'd broken all the other pairs and if we went in now he'd be sure to think that we'd come to take the last pair. But I tell you what – we could leave all his things on the doorstep, give a good loud knock and then hide round the corner until we were sure that he'd got them."

"Good idea. Let's hang them on the door-knob and then he's bound to see them if he opens the door at all."

As soon as they were all safely hanging on the knob, Sally went off to hide just round the corner of the house. Sandy gave three very loud knocks with the knocker and then hurried round the corner. A moment later, peeping cautiously round, though there was not much risk of being seen as there was little enough light left in the alley by now, they saw the door being slowly opened, an inch or two at a time. They caught just a glimpse of the tip of a pointed beard and then the door slammed shut again, but when they came out from their hiding-place everything had gone from the door-knob.

"Well, that's that," Sandy said.

"What do we do next?"

"Get back to *Dutchman* as quick as we jolly well can, or there'll be trouble."

"Here you are at last," their father greeted them, as they reached the edge of the quay. "I was just beginning to think I would have to send for the fire-engine. I suppose you realize what time it is, and I suppose you also realize, Miss Sally, that you ought to be safely tucked up in bed by now. We'll have to be off bright and early in the morning if I'm to get back in time to do a day's work."

"Daddy."

"Well, child, what is it you're wanting now, because whatever it is you can't have it."

"It wasn't me so much as – well – you I was thinking about. What was that you were saying the other day about ruts?" Sally went on.

"I'm quite sure I never said anything about ruts."

"Didn't you? Somehow I thought you did. Not that it matters really. Are they good things or bad things?"

"Bad things I should say. Quite definitely bad things – like tram-lines."

"Why like tram-lines?"

"Because once you get into them it's not very easy to get

out of them again and you just have to go where they take you."

"You know, Mummy, I think Daddy's looking just the tiniest little bit like a tram-car, don't you?"

"Well, I don't know. He doesn't seem to be making tram-car noises if that's what you mean."

"Not exactly."

"Well, what did you mean?"

"You know – in a sort of a rut – I mean all this about starting back very early in the morning so that he can do a good day's work. Don't you think he ought to have a few more days' rest?"

"And now," her father interrupted, "I begin to understand what all this is about. After beginning carefully at the end you now seem to have got round to the beginning. What you really want to know is whether we can stay on *Dutchman* a bit longer instead of going home."

"Oh no, it wasn't that at all, not really. It was just that I was thinking it wouldn't be very nice if people began saying to me, 'I think your Daddy is getting more like a tram-car every day.' That's all. It wasn't me I was thinking of at all. I tell you what. Let's spin a coin. Heads we stay and tails we don't. That would be quite fair, wouldn't it?"

Now Sally sometimes had rather strange ideas about what was fair and what was not, and as they all knew this quite well they looked at her with some suspicion.

"Some witchery going on here, I suspect," her father said. "Do we have to use a special penny of yours that always comes down the way you want?"

"Not at all. We can use one of your pennies and Mummy can spin it."

"All right. Heads we stay and tails we don't, is that it?"

A penny was produced and set spinning on the flat top of the engine cover. As it began to settle, they could all see that it was going to come tails.

When it finally came to rest Sally leant over it, and when she saw that it was tails she jumped up, clapping her hands with joy.

"Hooray, hooray, I've won! Jolly good!"

They all looked at her with some surprise, because they all thought the agreement was that they would stay longer if it was heads, but that if it was tails they would go home.

"Now wait a minute," said their father, scratching his head in a puzzled way. "I thought I said heads we stay and tails we don't."

"Yes, you did, and it's tails so we don't."

"Don't stay, you mean."

"Oh, good gracious no! That wasn't at all what I meant. I meant heads we stay and tails we don't go home. What's wrong with that? It's perfectly fair, isn't it? It was your penny and Mummy spun it so there can't possibly have been any cheating, can there?"

"I think," said her mother, "that feminine cunning has won the day, and it may be that your father will graciously admit defeat – but on one condition only."

"What?" asked Sally.

"That you are tucked up in your bunk in not more than one minute and five seconds from – now."

It was her father who had answered her question and as he did so he began to look at the second-hand of his watch. Sally was off to the forepeak in a flash and with less than three-quarters of a minute gone she was calling back, "I'm in bed now, and I have won, haven't I?"

CHAPTER TEN

They Find a Duck-Punt

Very early next morning Sandy pushed his head out from under the awning, and to his great surprise he saw that Sally was sitting in the dinghy.

"What on earth are you doing?" he asked.

"Sh!" Sally answered. "You'll wake the others. I'm going exploring. Coming?"

"All right, just a second."

They had soon cast off. Overhead the sky was blue, but down on the water lay a thick white mist, so thick that when they had pulled away two or three strokes the land had entirely vanished.

They moved slowly downstream, keeping, as best they could judge, to the middle of the river. The sound of the blades as they dipped into the water was completely deadened, and for a moment they had a strange impression that the little dinghy was a sledge on velvet runners sliding across an immense sea of steaming black ice.

"What's the matter?" Sandy asked, as Sally stopped rowing and leant on the oar handles.

"I just thought I heard something, but I must have imagined it."

"Let's keep quiet a minute and see if it comes again."

And come it did, more distinctly this time, a voice which was neither talking nor singing, but which seemed to be trying to sing without very much idea of tune, a flat, half-cracked, broken kind of voice.

Dipping one of the oars into the water, Sally swung the dinghy's head round.

"Shovelling salamanders!" she suddenly exclaimed. "Do you hear what he's trying to sing? The tune's all wrong, but the words are right."

Despite the cracked and wavering voice there could be no mistaking the words.

"Perry merry dixi, dominee,
Perry merry dixi, dominee."

"Hold her there," said Sandy. "I think I can just see something. It looks like a boat-house."

The mist had thinned momentarily to give a clear view of the gable end of a wooden boat-house, its doors open to the river, and lying within it was a strange-looking craft.

Then the mist closed in again, but not before Sandy had caught a glimpse of a figure.

"It's him all right, old Corny!"

"What's he doing?"

"I couldn't see. Let's wait around a bit and see what happens."

They sat there for maybe five minutes listening to the cracked voice trying to sing, and then all fell silent.

"I think he must have gone," said Sandy. "Let's go in a little closer."

They moved slowly in towards the open doors, which were wide enough to let the dinghy through.

"What an extraordinary boat," said Sally.

Sandy recognized it at once. It was an old and very large duck-punt of the kind used by fenland fowlers. It was painted a dull greyish green, and near the bows in a slightly different shade of green was the name – *Fen Tiger*.

Two odd things immediately caught Sandy's attention. The first was an extraordinary gun. The barrel, which pointed forwards over the bows, must have been all of eight feet long, and at the other end the heavy wooden stock was held in a device that looked rather like a sling made of canvas and rope. Sandy realized that this was meant to give the marksman some protection against the violent recoil that such a very big gun was bound to give. The metal was dull, no doubt deliberately so, in order to avoid catching a glint of sunlight, but it looked as if it might well have come from the gunsmith's only the day before.

The second thing he noticed was that, unlike any duck-punt he had ever seen, this one had an engine fitted – a steam-engine of all things, complete with fire-box, boiler, smoke-stack, pressure-gauge and all. Now the curious thing was that while everything possible had been done to camouflage the boat itself, as well as the gun, the brass smoke-stack and all the copper-work of the engine had been polished till they shone brilliantly. It was as though the owner of the boat had known quite well that a duck-punt, if it was to serve its purpose, should be made as nearly invisible as possible, but at the same time he had been so proud of his engine that he could not bear to see the least speck of dirty brass anywhere.

The boat itself had all the appearance of having been lately got ready for a voyage. Close by the fire-box lay a newspaper, a box of matches, some pieces of dry stick and a small sack which looked rather as if it might contain coal, and near the stern there was a wicker basket which probably contained provisions. And there was another object that puzzled the children. It was rather bulky and it lay, carefully wrapped in a groundsheet, on a thwart that was just aft of the engine.

"What do you think it can be?" Sandy asked Sally. And for answer, to his great alarm, she climbed out of the dinghy into the duck-punt and proceeded to remove the groundsheet from the object which it was covering.

Beneath the cover was a book of immense size. Its pages must have measured nearly two feet from top to bottom and about a foot across and it looked very old. Certainly it was very heavy and even Sally did not dare try to pick it up.

"Come on," said Sandy impatiently. "Wrap it up again and make sure it was just as you found it, but don't be too long about it."

"Just a second. I wonder what this is – looks like a bookmarker of some sort. Just let me have a look at the page it's marking."

She turned the pages carefully over until she came to the marker, and as she let the book lie open Sandy could see that on one side there was heavy black lettering that looked like Latin, and facing on the other side was a painting of a flowering plant.

He just had time to read the name of the plant when he heard the sound of approaching footsteps.

"Quick, he's coming back! Jump in! There's no time to wrap it up again, you'll just have to leave it as it is."

He moved quickly to the oars. Sally jumped in over the stern and they slipped out through the door just as a small door opened at the landward end of the boat-house. Fortunately the mist was still fairly thick and the dinghy was soon completely hidden. Suddenly out of the mist and from the direction of the boat-house there came a high-pitched scream.

"Wizards – witches – they're after me. To arms! To arms!"

A few seconds later there came an explosion that must have startled the jackdaws away up at the top of the cathedral tower. Poor Sally nearly jumped out of the boat with fright.

"What on earth was that?" she asked.

"I fancy that was old Corny firing his gun so as to frighten away the wizards and witches. I hope he doesn't load it with nails. Anyway, we don't seem to have been hit. By the way, did you happen to see what was the name of that flower on the page where the marker was?"

"No, I didn't. Did you?"

"Yes."

"What was it?"

"*Helleborus viridis.*"

"What do you think it all means?" Sally asked.

"It looks fairly obvious to me what it means. The old Professor thinks that you and I have bewitched him. Remember he doesn't know anything about Pout, at least not more than some old legend about him singing the song in the park on winter nights, and he thinks we broke all his spectacles. Well, you remember what our own flower book says about Green Hellebore, how people used to use it for breaking witches' spells. My guess is that he's got his duck-punt all ready to go off on an expedition and that the purpose of the expedition is to find some Green Hellebore to break the spells he thinks we've put on him."

"I wonder if you're right. I hope you are."

"Why? It doesn't make much difference to us that I can see."

"Of course it does, you gormless gowk – I mean you dearest and kindest of brothers. Don't you see? Pout wants Green Hellebore to help him get Cerberus back, and old

Candlesnuffer wants it to break our spells. All we've got to do is to follow the Professor, and if we can keep on his tracks long enough he will probably lead us to some place where Green Hellebore is growing – and then perhaps we'll be able to find Cerberus."

CHAPTER ELEVEN

The Chase Begins

"It's an idea," Sandy remarked, as they pulled back to *Dutchman*, "but I'm not sure that I believe in Cerberus."

"I suppose you'll be saying next that you don't believe in Pout either, or the Professor."

"Oh, the Professor's real enough, but it's not going to be easy to follow him."

"I've got it! Let's have a mutiny and capture the ship."

"But I thought it was our ship already."

"So it is, but if we mutinied you could be captain instead of Daddy – and I would give the orders."

"I always thought it was the captain who gave the orders."

"My mutiny's going to be different. I don't see why we should be like everyone else."

"Supposing," said Sandy, after thinking for a moment, "supposing old Corny goes the other way."

"He won't."

"How do you know?"

"Something to do with Great-aunt Tryphena, I suppose."

"Well, how do we set about capturing the ship?"

"That's easy, we just take her away."

"Without waking Mummy and Daddy?"

"You just leave that to me."

"You're not serious, are you?"

"Of course I am. We've got to find some Green Hellebore somehow and I don't suppose Daddy will let us stay all that much longer."

The whole thing seemed absolutely crazy to Sandy, but he knew how determined his sister could be when she really wanted something.

"Get the engine ready," Sally whispered, as they climbed back aboard *Dutchman*.

While Sandy worked on the engine, Sally jumped on to the quay and loosened the mooring ropes. She eased the head rope so that *Dutchman*'s bows could swing out into the river. Then, leaning with all her weight against the ship's side to push her clear, she jumped aboard again.

"Shall I start her up?" Sandy asked anxiously. "We'll look pretty silly mutineers if we just go drifting about the river bumping into people."

"No, I haven't dealt with the prisoners yet."

Moving as quietly as only she knew how, Sally went into the cabin and came out a moment or two later with finger to lips to stop Sandy's question.

"All right, you can start her now," she said.

"How far are we going?" Sandy asked.

"It's no good asking me. You're the captain and the captain gives the orders."

"But I thought you said you were going to give the orders."

"Did I? Well, I jolly well wouldn't take orders from a girl if I were you."

"Well, hang it all, it was your idea, all this mutiny stuff."

"Do you know," said Sally, with a stretch and a yawn, "I think I'm feeling rather sleepy. In fact I think I'm going back to bed."

"Hey! But you can't do that! What on earth am I going to do and where am I going to stop?"

"Oh, that's your business. After all, you are the captain, aren't you?"

She was already halfway along the deck and soon she had disappeared down the forehatch to her bunk, leaving Sandy alone in charge of the ship.

And what, he thought to himself, was he going to do next? His father and mother would certainly wake up sooner or later and what then? And then he had a sudden idea. If three people could sleep down below, then why not four?

He began to look around to see if there was a likely place where he could bring *Dutchman* safely to the bank single-handed. The flood banks were set well back from the river itself and that should make it easier. There was no wind and scarcely any current.

He slipped the engine into neutral and left the wheel to look after itself while he got the two anchors ready. By good luck, or as he preferred to think, by good judgment, he managed to get *Dutchman* alongside exactly where he wanted her. He made her fast to the bank and turned the engine off. A few minutes later, not yet six o'clock by his watch, he was in his sleeping-bag with the awning pulled back over the well.

The next thing that Sandy knew was that his father was standing in the well looking out from under the awning.

"Can't understand what's going on," he muttered.

The children's mother came out of the cabin to see what the trouble was.

"Curious, very curious," she remarked.

"Has something exciting happened?" asked Sally, joining the others.

"That is a matter of opinion," her father replied, "on which I am not prepared to pronounce at the moment, but I have a very distinct feeling that when I went to bed last night, the cathedral was much nearer than it appears to be at the moment. And how quickly the grass seems to have grown."

"That's nothing to worry about," said Sally.

"When you reach my age you will find it a little disturbing to meet with quite such unexpected changes. The weather, by all means – but cathedrals, and in fact whole towns, ought not to move about in the middle of the night."

"Tram-lines," said Sally.

"I beg your pardon?"

"Nothing. I just said 'tram-lines'. It's – it's – well, it's a sort of expression, like 'stuttering siskins'."

"Really, Sally," said her mother, "you do seem to get hold of the most extraordinary expressions these days. What sort of company have you been keeping lately?"

"I don't know what you're all worrying about," Sally went on. "It's quite obvious what's happened."

"Perhaps you would explain – preferably in words of one syllable."

"You all seem to think that *Dutchman* stopped at Ely last night, but what really happened was that Ely stopped at *Dutchman* and now it's moved on again. That's all."

"In that case," said her father, "I hereby announce to all and sundry that I lay down my commission and resign my command of the good ship *Dutchman*."

"Hooray, hooray!" shouted Sally. "Then Sandy and I can take over."

At that moment a strange sound reached them from away down the river – three blasts on a steam-whistle. Sandy and his sister looked at each other for a moment, each understanding what it was.

"Looks like rain to me," she said. "We'd better get the awning over."

"But ... "

"It's no good, Mummy, we're in command now. Into the cabin with both of you. You might get wet."

Needless to say, there was not so much as a wisp of cloud to be seen in the sky.

If the children had gone into the cabin they might have heard some remarks pass between their father and mother.

"I'm not quite sure that I like this," their father said.

"Trouble, do you think?"

"Could be."

"You don't think there's any – well – danger – do you?"

"I just have a feeling that they're getting mixed up in something they don't quite understand – that professor chap – and these strange expressions – I'm sure they didn't make them up themselves."

"Ought we ask them, do you think?"

"No, I think better not. They'd never say. We'd best just go along with them, and keep our eyes open. It was Sally coming into the cabin this morning and trying to sort of mesmerize us that's got me a bit worried. We'll just have to wait and see."

Now *Dutchman* was lying near the upper end of a longish and fairly straight reach, perhaps not more than a quarter of a mile from the old inn where the river forked, and Sandy saw that from where they were they would be able to see which fork *Fen Tiger* was taking. At the moment she was giving her position away by a tall column of black smoke which trailed behind her across the blue sky and which suggested that the fire had recently been stoked.

"We'd better be ready to take cover in a minute," Sandy

said. "He'll be round the corner soon and we mustn't let him see us."

The children arranged the awning so that they could both look out through the slit at the stern, and in a moment or two they saw what was indeed a most splendid and impressive sight. Low down in the water, the great gun pointing straight ahead over her bows, thick black smoke belching from her smoke-stack, *Fen Tiger* came creaming up the river, shearing it apart, for all the world like some naval frigate making full speed at sea, and setting up a great bow wave that broke through the reeds and over the washlands behind her. A flock of geese that had been peacefully grazing took swiftly to flight with much raucous quacking as the unexpected flood overtook them. Surely no duck-punt had ever moved through the water like this before. As the children looked there came a wisp of steam, white against the black smoke from the funnel, and a split second later the sound of the whistle reached them across the water – again it came – and a third time.

It was like a weird and wonderful aquatic fire-engine, shrieking with its whistle to clear everyone from its path and raising every ounce of steam till the pressure-gauge must surely have been well beyond the danger mark.

And then as they watched *Fen Tiger* the great bow wave was suddenly stilled, and the ship herself sheered off towards the further bank, disappearing from sight in a cloud of white steam.

"What's happened?" Sally asked. "Has she blown up?"

"I think I know what it is," said Sandy. "He's got near enough to be able to recognize *Dutchman* and he's pulled into the bank to let the pressure out of the boiler. I expect that means that he's going to try to get past us without our seeing him. We'll have to keep well under cover now."

Just at that moment there came a voice from the cabin. "May we come out? It's getting a bit warm here."

"Certainly not," said Sally. "It might be very dangerous. If you're very careful not to be seen you can look out through one of the port-holes, but you must be absolutely quiet.

"Look. She's beginning to move again," she added.

And so she was, but very, very slowly. Close by the farther shore, almost brushing against the reeds, she nosed her way along, but looking now a completely different ship. The shining brass smoke-stack had gone and Sandy guessed that it must have been pulled down rather as a tugboat will pull hers down when she has to pass beneath a low bridge. The boiler and all the shining copper pipes had likewise gone from view, covered up by some sort of dark-green sailcloth out of which, at odd angles, there projected an assortment of reeds and sedges and teazles, so that the stern half, if one looked at it with the eye of a duck, might perhaps resemble a floating island.

"She's been cleared for action and camouflaged, that's what it is," said Sandy. "For goodness' sake keep well covered. We don't want to be shot at again with that gun."

Slowly, slowly *Fen Tiger* crept along the bank, and if the reeds had been just that much thicker she would have been very well hidden. She was scarcely fifty yards away now, and they were still greatly mystified to know how she was moving along, because it was obvious that the engine could not be in use. Then as she came closer she sheered away from the bank again and for a while she was headed directly towards them so that they were looking straight at the mouth of that wicked gun-barrel. Then they saw what it was that was moving her through the water.

Though the rest of him could not easily be distinguished, Professor Candlewick's two arms, enveloped in dark green sleeves, were stretched out one over each side of the boat, and in each hand he held a small paddle. It was with these paddles that he was slowly working *Fen Tiger* along. Closer and closer he came – forty – thirty – twenty yards – pausing every now and again to make sure that he had not been heard.

On he came and the children hardly dared to breathe. Now he was within two or three yards and still making straight towards *Dutchman*. And now he was near enough for both of them to get a clear view. He was lying stretched out at full length, flat on his stomach – as flat, that is, as was possible for such a very round man. His legs lay straight out behind him, his arms were over the side with their paddles, and his head low down behind the butt of the great gun, so that scarcely anything of him showed above the gunwale except for his two arms.

It was his head that made them both catch their breath when they first got a clear view of it. It was covered with the most remarkable hat that either of them had ever seen, made – believe it or not – of the skin of a large hedgehog with all the bristles still attached. Over his forehead there protruded the little black hedgehog's snout and above the snout were two beady, black eyes. Down his cheek there hung the creature's forepaws. Of his face itself they could see next to nothing save for the shining gold rims and the moon-like lenses of his spectacles, which now and again caught a glint of sunlight and sent it flashing back like twin signalling-lamps.

Still he came on, creeping up close beneath *Dutchman*'s stern, edging silently alongside and so passing out of sight. Without saying a word the children made their way back into the cabin.

With fingers on lips to impress on their father and mother the need for silence, they sat down on a bunk and waited, wondering what was going to happen next. For a full minute they sat there in absolute silence, a minute that seemed to stretch for an hour.

Then their mother looked up from her book and seemed

to freeze quite motionless – her mouth hanging open, her eyes rounded with astonishment and a look of the utmost alarm and horror upon her face. She seemed quite unable to move, and then suddenly the tension was shattered as she let out a piercing scream.

"Help – thieves – pirates – murderers – hedgehogs – quick – my smelling-salts – brandy – anything – but don't let me see it again!"

Then she collapsed on the bunk in a fit of hysterical laughter. It was some minutes before she was able to speak.

"What on earth is the matter?" one of them asked. "Have you seen a ghost or something?"

"Worse – much worse – my smelling salts again!"

"Well – what was it? Do hurry up and tell us!"

"I can't believe it, but I know it was there. I saw it plainly, even though I have only got two and it had four."

"What are you talking about? For goodness' sake tell us!"

"A hedgehog – there – looking in at the port-hole – a hedgehog – I know it was!"

"Well, what's so terrible about that?" asked the children's father in a disappointed voice. "There are lots of hedgehogs about, and I expect one of them climbed on during the night and got lost trying to find his way off again."

"No, no! It's not that. I don't mind hedgehogs – not ordinary ones."

"What was so terrible about this one?"

"It has – it had – oh dear – don't let me see it again – it had two pairs of eyes and the bottom pair was wearing gold-rimmed spectacles."

CHAPTER TWELVE

On the Trail

"Is nobody ever going to look outside to see if that monster is still there?"

"It's all right, Mummy, I expect he'll have gone by now – if he was ever there," said Sally, giving her brother a meaning look.

"I'll go and see," said Sandy.

He pushed his head out under the awning, as though afraid of what he might see – as indeed he was, because, for all he knew, *Fen Tiger* might still be there. But there was nothing at all to be seen, save the tail end of the duck-punt just disappearing round the far bend of the river. He beckoned to Sally and the two had a few whispered words together.

"You two are to stay there," she said to their mother and father. "We're off to do some scouting round, and don't forget we're in charge now."

They made their way quickly across the grass to the flood-bank, scrambled over it and down the other side and then walked along towards the thin column of smoke that they guessed must be coming from *Fen Tiger*'s funnel. After a few hundred yards the flood-bank began to curve round and they knew that they must have reached the place where the river forked.

"Better go carefully here," said Sandy.

They dropped down on hands and knees and wriggled cautiously up to the top, keeping their heads low down. And there down below them, moored to the landing-stage by the old inn, lay *Fen Tiger*, all her camouflage gone, her brass smoke-stack gleaming in the sun and the great gun pointing forward over her bows.

A moment or two later Professor Candlewick came out of the inn. He no longer wore his hedgehog hat, but the great gold-rimmed spectacles were still there, and he looked anxiously about him as he hurried back to his duck-punt. Once aboard, he gave three toots on his steam-whistle and was off up the river.

"What do we do next?" said Sandy.

"Give chase, of course, and we'd better be quick about it."

The children ran back to *Dutchman* as fast as they could go.

"You get her going and I'll cast off," called Sally, as they jumped aboard.

"You know," said her father who had been sitting thoughtfully watching operations, "there's one thing that's puzzling me a little. Are we running away from something or are we chasing something? I don't much like running away but I'm all for the fun of the chase."

"Chasing," said Sandy.

"Good, and if it's not too great a secret would you mind telling us just what we're chasing?"

"*Fen Tiger.*"

"What???" Sandy's mother almost shrieked. "Did I understand you to say that after having narrowly escaped being boarded and eaten alive by a ravening horde of four-eyed hedgehogs with gold-rimmed glasses we are now in hot pursuit of a tiger?"

"Sounds exciting," said father. "And exactly which way did this fen tiger go?"

"That's the trouble. He went up the river, but we don't know whether he'll keep to the river or turn off into the lode. What do you think we ought to do, Mummy?" Sandy asked.

"Go home, of course – at once."

"What do you say, Daddy?"

"When in doubt stick to the rules. That's what I say."

"Does all that mean that we ought to begin with rule one?" Sally asked.

"You have understood my meaning with a promptness which would have brought pleasure to your celebrated great-aunt Tryphena."

"Never take any notice of what people say."

"And what has prompted you to give your father such excellent advice?"

"Rule one. You said begin at the beginning, so I have. That's it, rule one, I mean."

"Oh – and does it help?"

"Well, yes, I think it does. We asked Mummy first and she wanted to go home and rule one means that we don't take any notice of what she says."

"I fancy," said her mother, "this is by no means the first time that I have suffered from the application of rule one."

"And what next?"

"Rule two, of course – the longest way round is the shortest way home."

"And does that help?" her father asked. "Such obvious nonsense must be full of most profound wisdom."

"Just let me think for a minute."

"Well, don't think for too long," said Sandy, "because if we're going to go up the lode we'll have to turn pretty soon."

"I believe it does help," said Sally. "We can't possibly go home till we've found him, and according to rule two the quickest way of getting home should be to take the longest way round, and that can only mean going back up the lode. Come on, round we go! I'm sure that's right."

And a few minutes later they were through the lock among the bobbing water-lilies, but their problem was only one stage towards solution. There were still three ways open to *Fen Tiger*.

Then Sandy suddenly remembered the cock-up bridge, an old, hump-backed and rather decrepit wooden bridge that spanned the mouth of Wicken lode, the first of the three turnings that *Fen Tiger* could have taken. It was built high above the water, to allow sedge-laden barges to pass underneath, and from its top there was a wide view across the fen clear away to the chalk ridge at whose foot the old villages lay. If there was any smoke coming from *Fen Tiger* they could not fail to see it.

As soon as they had got *Dutchman* up to the bank they went ashore, taking binoculars with them. They climbed up to the top of the rickety bridge and looked about for any signs that they could see. Slowly they scanned the whole fen. Close at hand was the clump of poplars growing on Pout Hall Fen, and even without the binoculars it was possible to pick out the old windmill and the church towers cutting the skyline, but of their quarry there was no sign at all.

"I think we must have lost him," said Sandy disappointedly.

Neither boats nor living creatures could he see, save the peewits diving and tumbling above the fen.

"Come on, it's no good. We'd better go back to *Dutchman*

and think what we ought to do next. Perhaps it would be best to ask the lock-keeper after all."

"Wait a minute," said Sally. "Let's think for a bit. Don't you remember what Pout said that night you came tumbling down the bank, about getting there much more quickly if you weren't in such a hurry?"

"That sounds pretty much the same as rule two and we've followed that, but it doesn't seem to be working very well."

"I wonder. Suppose we take Daddy's advice and go on sticking to the rules. After all, one and two have brought us here. What was rule three?"

"I think it was something about never starting something you can't stop."

"That doesn't sound very helpful. What was four?"

"Oh, that was a stupid one about not spoiling the soup for a pinch of pepper. I don't think he meant that one very seriously."

"And that only leaves five – never do anything yourself if you can get someone else to do it for you – I don't see how that can help us, because there isn't anyone else here.

"I wish I could remember something," Sally went on in a thoughtful voice as she stood looking over the edge of the bridge at the fish swimming about in the water below. "It was something that Pout said, and I have a feeling that it might be important if only I could remember what it was."

"Just look at those peewits over there." Sandy had his glasses focused on them as they came tumbling and swooping down over the fen near the clump of popular trees. "You can hear them calling and they sound quite angry."

"Oh, stop burbling about peewits when I'm trying hard to remember whatever it is that I've forgotten."

"They're just like dive-bombers. When did he say it? Out on the fen or on top of the hill?"

"I think it was on the hill and I'm sure it had something to do with rule five. I've got it! He said that people often make the mistake of thinking they're alone when there's nobody there, and it was after that that he told us how he got Loppy Lugs to move and start dripping water down the tower."

"Well Loppy Lugs isn't here now and I don't see anyone else that looks like him."

"The peewits! Of course. Why on earth didn't you think of them before!"

"Well. I like that! After you told me to stop burbling about them. What can they do anyway?"

"The way they're diving down at the same place all the time. Don't hedgehogs steal eggs? Supposing they'd got a nest somewhere over there, the peewits I mean, and supposing they'd caught sight of the Professor's hedgehog hat hanging out to dry."

"You seem to be doing an awful lot of supposing. I don't see why his hedgehog hat should be hanging out to dry, anyway. It hasn't rained today."

"Oh, don't be stupid. It doesn't matter whether it's rained or not. Give me those glasses for a moment."

Sally took them and looked long and hard at the peewits and the poplar trees, and then suddenly let out an excited little cry.

"I do believe I'm right. I must be right. I'm always right. Close behind the poplar trees down there – they're blowing about just a little and I'm sure I caught a glimpse of something gleaming behind them."

"Let me see."

Sandy took the binoculars back and after taking a careful look he began to think that perhaps she was right after all. There did seem to be something glinting in the sun, and it could perhaps be *Fen Tiger*'s smoke-stack, which would be just high enough to show above the bank of the lode. It was just there too that the peewits were diving. Again and again they came, always back to the same place. Perhaps it was rule five working and perhaps the peewits were finding *Fen Tiger* for them. The Professor would never think of being given away by birds.

CHAPTER THIRTEEN

The Strange Behaviour of Professor Candlewick

It was a chance, and it was certainly worth going to have a closer look, if only they could manage to get somewhere near without being seen.

If they were right, *Fen Tiger* must have taken the right-hand fork – Reach Lode, that would be – and it looked as if he must have pulled into the bank just a little way past the junction. With luck they might be able to get back to their old moorings. Then, in between *Dutchman* and *Fen Tiger*, there would be the little triangular patch of Pout Hall Fen, with its growth of thorn bushes and the clump of poplars, and perhaps that would give them the cover they needed.

Sandy began to get a little anxious as they approached the fork, because, if *Fen Tiger* was there, there was just a chance that they might come within sight of one another for a brief moment; but all was well. They passed the critical point without seeing any sign of either the Professor or the boat, and they made fast once more at the identical spot where they had moored the first night. Somehow it seemed right that the chase should have brought them back just there.

Was *Fen Tiger* really lying in the other lode or had they been misled by something else glinting in the sunlight? They could answer that question easily enough by going to have a look, but would it be wise in broad daylight? In the end they decided that the best plan would be to wait till they had had lunch, and then for one of them to cross over the bank down into the fen and go just far enough to be able to get a view along the other lode, so as to discover whether he was really there or not. It was Sally who eventually went, and it seemed an age till Sandy caught sight of her coming back again. She gave a little nod as soon as he saw her and he knew at once that all was well.

"It's all right," she said, when they were both back aboard *Dutchman* and sitting up on the foredeck. "He's there."

"Did you see him?"

"Well, no, I didn't actually see the Professor himself, but I saw *Fen Tiger*."

"How do you know he's there if you didn't see him? He might have left the boat and gone off walking somewhere."

"I don't think so. He would never have gone off and left his hedgehog hat like that. There was quite a tall stick pushed into the ground on the bank just by *Fen Tiger* and his hedgehog hat was balanced on the top of it. Why do you think he'd done that?"

"Oh, to scare away the witches, I should think. I believe I've read somewhere about people putting the heads of animals on the top of poles to frighten away witches and devils and that sort of thing."

"Well, I'm sure he would never have left it. It must be

one of his best treasures, I should think, especially if he thinks it's any good against witchcraft."

"Perhaps you were right about the peewits after all. I wonder if he's going to stay there all night."

"I tell you what. You've only got to go quite a short way to get a glimpse of *Fen Tiger* through the bushes. Supposing one of us was to go every now and then just to make sure that he's still there."

"Good idea."

And that was what they did. Their father and mother stayed aboard, watching perhaps a little more closely than the children realized.

It was after supper that Sandy began to wonder if it might be worth while trying to get a little nearer. So far they had no idea about what the Professor's plans were and perhaps a closer inspection might tell them something. A slight breeze had sprung up, enough to set the poplar leaves rustling, which would help to cover up any slight sounds they might make.

Telling the others to remember that they were to regard themselves as captives and were on no account to leave the boat, the children made their way once more up and over the bank and past the thickets of hawthorn. This time, instead of making for the point that they had been using during the afternoon to spy on *Fen Tiger*, they laid off a different course which they reckoned would bring them fairly close and at the same time give them good cover.

The going was slow because there was always the risk of treading on a dry stick, but eventually they reached their target undiscovered. If they had judged it right, *Fen Tiger* should be lying over the bank and perhaps about fifteen yards away to the left. Then it was a matter of wriggling up to the top. Inch by inch they wormed their way up and as they reached the top they parted the grasses so that they could peer through without raising their heads.

Fen Tiger was there all right, but not the fifteen yards away that they had expected. Somehow they must have misjudged the direction, for there she was lying directly below them. A first glance suggested that she was not likely to move far that night. Over the whole boat was stretched a dark-green awning, curiously shaped so that it rose up steeply from bow and stern to reach its highest point more or less amidships. There appeared to be two holes in the awning. One was up at the bows, and out of it they could see the muzzle of the gun protruding for some six inches. The other hole was amidships and had been shaped to allow the smoke-stack to project above it, and it was the top few inches above the awning that they had seen glinting in the sun.

The grass on the bank below seemed to have been much trampled, but of Professor Candlewick himself they could see no sign and they began to wonder where he could be. His hedgehog hat was still there on the top of the pole, like some curious battle-standard. They just lay and watched, not daring so much as to whisper. Then *Fen Tiger* suddenly began to rock from side to side, sending ripples across the lode. For the most part she rocked gently, but now and again she gave a violent lurch, so much so that once or twice she looked almost like overturning. It was then that they realized where the Professor must be, but what he was doing was more than they could imagine.

After a while the rocking ceased and a moment later a hand came out through a slit in the canvas, which it proceeded to fold back a little way. The hand was followed by a shining brass helmet, which looked like, and perhaps was, an old coal-scuttle.

Beneath the helmet they caught a glimpse of the familiar gold-rimmed spectacles and soon the whole of him was standing there on the bank below them in all his full splendour. Below helmet, spectacles and pointed beard, he wore a magnificent scarlet-coloured coat and below his scarlet coat his trousers – or rather his breeches, since they came down only to his knee, where they were tucked into woollen stockings – were of a no less magnificently brilliant blue.

Why on earth had he got himself up in this finery? Did he imagine himself to be a sentry, on duty outside Buckingham Palace? Or was he just showing off his splendid clothes to the evening sky? Certainly he looked rather like a peacock strutting up and down the bank. He would stump off a few paces in one direction and then he would turn about and come back a few paces in the opposite direction. For perhaps ten minutes the display went on until finally he stumped up to the stick, removed from it the hedgehog hat and went back aboard *Fen Tiger*, which began once more to rock from side to side. Evidently he was taking off his elegant clothes.

In a little while the rocking stopped and all was still once more. A moment later the awning took on a luminous hue and they guessed that he must have lit a lantern. They stayed a while longer, but nothing more happened, and it looked as if he had finally turned in for the night, though it was still rather early to be going to bed.

Then, breaking the silence, and sounding all the stranger for being muffled by the awning, came that cracked and tuneless voice.

"Perry merry dixi, dominee."

After that complete silence.

"Well, did you find your tiger?" It was their father who put the question later in the evening.

"Yes, we found him all right," Sandy replied.

"By strict application to the rules, no doubt?"

"More or less."

"Good. I thought they might work. And what do you

propose to do next, if it's not prying too much into state secrets?"

"I don't know exactly."

"What did he look like when you found him?"

"Very odd indeed."

"Yes," Sally joined in. "It wasn't quite what I'd expected."

"Things seldom are. And what was peculiar?"

"His clothing. You see, his coat was red and his trousers were blue."

"Were they now? That strikes me as very interesting. And was there by any chance a hole where the tail came through?"

"Don't be silly. Of course there wasn't."

"I can assure you that I am not being in the least silly. When I hear a daughter of mine talking about a strange character wearing a red coat and blue trousers I begin to wonder if maybe she is meddling with something that she does not wholly understand. The trouble is that people don't read enough poetry nowadays."

"What's that got to do with it?"

"His jacket was red and his breeches were blue
And there was a hole where the tail came through."

"That's nice," said Sally. "Who wrote it, what's it about and how does it go on?"

"A poet called Coleridge wrote it. I forget how it goes on, but I remember well enough what it's about."

"What?"

"The devil. And I can also remember how it begins."

"How? Do tell us."

"From his brimstone bed at break of day
A-walking the devil is gone."

CHAPTER FOURTEEN

Sandy has Doubts

"I wonder how all this is going to end," Sandy said to Sally later in the evening. "Sometimes I think that perhaps we ought not to go on with it."

"Why not? I don't see that we've done anything wrong."

"That's not exactly what I meant."

"What don't you like about it?"

"All this about Green Hellebore and witchcraft and Professor Candlewick dressing up in those odd clothes. I don't know what you thought, but it sounded to me as if Daddy was – well, a bit worried. I noticed him looking at you in a strange way. We don't want to get mixed up in a lot of black magic."

"Surely you don't think witchcraft can do people any harm, do you? I think you're frightened, that's what I think."

"Well, what if I am? Other people have been frightened by witchcraft before now. In fact I believe people have been killed by it. We seem to have started something and I'm not sure that it isn't time that we stopped before it's too late."

"I don't think we can. I know I can't. I've simply got to find out what's going to happen."

"Perhaps we ought to tell Mummy and Daddy."

"On no, we couldn't possibly do that. They'd pack up and go home at once."

"That might be the best thing."

"No it wouldn't. It would be the worst possible thing. I'd still have to find out somehow and you'd have to help. Don't you remember how Pout told us we'd have to go on helping whether we wanted to or not? It's – it's like – it's like running upstairs in the dark and you think there's someone coming up behind you. You can't walk, however hard you try. You've simply got to run as fast as you possibly can."

"Well, I don't see why we shouldn't be able to stop. After all, we didn't start it. It just started itself."

"I know it did and that's why it's got to go on until it finishes, whatever happens. He went to bed very early, didn't he? The Professor, I mean. I expect that means that he's going to start off very early in the morning, and so are we. Goodnight."

Sally went off to the forepeak and left Sandy with his thoughts. It was well enough to go chasing *Fen Tiger* like this, but that business of the hedgehog on the stick – there was something worrying about that. They might laugh at the Professor, and he certainly looked a comical figure, but strange tales were told about the fens, and people said that curious customs still lingered on in remote places. For all that great expanse of sky overhead there were times when you felt the presence of things more dark and menacing. You felt so small and insignificant beneath it all. Yet Sally would have her way. Sandy knew that well enough.

What did it all mean? Pout suddenly appearing like that – he seemed to have some great power inside him – and yet he seemed to be a sort of prisoner. Who was keeping him prisoner and why? And what would happen if he got free? And then old Professor Candlewick – he must have known something about Pout – he certainly knew the tune and the odd words – but surely he couldn't really believe that he and Sally were over six hundred years old?

As he lay thinking his thoughts, Sandy was reminded of an autumn night a little while ago. He had gone out into the garden after dark. The first chill breath of winter's frosts was stealing down from the northern hills, and overhead the stars blazed and sparkled with icy heat against the blackness of space. As he turned to look for the Plough, from the corner of his eye he caught a sudden glimpse of a star that shot halfway across the heavens almost before he had even seen it. Seen and yet not seen, powerful beyond imagining and yet utterly silent – the brief vision left him with a sense half of joy at the beauty of the night, half of fear at the immensity of the unknown. Was it good or evil? Or was it simply power that knew nothing of either good or evil? And why had Pout reminded him of this shooting star?

There was something that Pout had said about luck – good luck and bad luck. Was that what he really was? Not a person at all, not good, nor bad either, but just luck – just my luck. That's what people said sometimes – a bit like shooting stars, something that happened, or didn't happen, but it wasn't your fault whether it did or not.

It was all very puzzling, but there was no doubt that Sandy was a little frightened. And the sudden recollection that away up at the head of the lode there lay one end of the great earthwork that men called the Devil's Dyke did nothing to still his fears. However, there was nothing to be done about it. Best try to forget it all and go to sleep so as to be ready for whatever the morrow might bring.

Little did he think how long it was going to be before they were all together on *Dutchman* again.

CHAPTER FIFTEEN

The Quarrel

It seemed to be daylight again in no time. Sandy woke very early. He had slept soundly, but something of his fears still lingered. He pushed them out of his mind again as best he could, and very soon he and Sally were busy with the preparations for their expedition.

"There now," said Sally, "I think that's everything. Let's cast off."

"Just a minute. I believe I've forgotten something."

It was then that Sandy climbed from the dinghy and hastily scribbled a note which he addressed to his father and left on top of the primus. Why he did so, he could not tell. It was rather like Sally running upstairs in the dark. All he said was that they had gone after *Fen Tiger* to see if they could find some Green Hellebore. The message would hardly make much sense, but Sally was getting impatient and he did not want her to know what he was doing.

First they had to make their way back to the point where the two lodes joined. It did not occur to either of them that it might have been wiser to see whether *Fen Tiger* was still lying there. Perhaps they both knew, without knowing how they knew, that they would find her berth deserted. So indeed they did.

There was the trampled patch of grass near the water's edge, where the Professor had marched up and down in his ridiculous clothes. There too was the stick still standing upright in the ground, but there was no longer any hedgehog hat on top of it.

The morning was clear and bright, but there was already a coppery look about the air which suggested that a change might be coming, and a warm, slightly sultry breeze was blowing up from the south. That meant a beam wind for the little dinghy, so that the children could let the wind do all the work for them – up with the mast and sail, down with the centre-board, and there they were slipping nicely along at a good speed.

At that early hour they had the lode completely to themselves, with not even a fisherman to see them pass by. A hoarse cra-a-a-ack overhead made Sandy look up to see a heron fly over. With its great wings outspread to catch the wind it began to swing round in wide circles, higher and higher. The wind carried it slowly across the fens till it must have risen many hundreds of feet, and then suddenly, almost as though it had taken fright at being so high up, it came tumbling down again like a giant peewit, went off in a long shallow glide and was lost from sight.

Sandy's fears were forgotten in the joy of the sail, but all too soon, round a shallow bend, they saw that they had reached the head of the lode, and there before them, rising steeply above the fen, the chimney-stacks of the old houses stood up among the trees. Sandy wished the journey had been longer, but it was no good wishing. They had completed the first stage, and now they had to see if *Fen Tiger* was there.

As they got near the end of the lode they took the sail down, unstepped the little mast and began to make their way along with the oars, looking around them among the willows and the reeds. It did not take them long to find her, pushed a little way along what was really no more than a ditch. With her green awning pulled right over and tall reeds growing on either side, she was well hidden. They would certainly never have spotted her unless they had been deliberately looking.

"Well, that's the first step," Sandy said. "What do we do next?"

"Hide the dinghy somewhere and then see if we can pick up the trail. I bet he's gone along the dyke."

"What makes you think that?"

"Just that it seems so obvious. You remember the poem Daddy told us about and how it begun."

"Something about brimstone and the dawn."

"From his brimstone bed at break of day
A-walking the devil is gone."

"Yes, I remember it now, but how does it help?"

"Surely if the devil went for a walk just here, the obvious place for him to walk along would be his own dyke."

"Well, I suppose there may be something in that, but are you thinking that Professor Candlewick is really the devil in disguise?"

"No, not exactly. I think he's sort of pretending to be, but I don't quite understand why, unless he thinks it's the best way to defend himself against witchcraft. Anyway, there's another reason for going along the dyke. The flower book says that Green Hellebore mostly grows in woods on chalk or limestone."

"The chalk's easy enough to find. There's masses of it. In fact I believe it's all chalk from one end of the Devil's Dyke to the other, but I don't think there are any woods along the Dyke, not proper ones at least. We've walked along it often enough where it crosses the heath and the race-course, but there aren't any trees there at all."

"No, I know there aren't, but there's one place where there is a wood. At least there jolly well ought to be."

"How do you know?"

"Because I had a look at a map. In fact I thought it might be a good idea to bring one with us. Look at this."

Sally spread out the map and traced with her finger the long, straight line of the Devil's Dyke till she reached its farthermost end.

"Look there," she said. "That belt of green, doesn't that mean trees?"

"Yes, it ought to, unless the trees have been cut down since the map was made."

"It's a new map. Daddy got it only the other day. There they are then, all three together, chalk, a wood and the Devil's Dyke. I bet you anything you like that's where the Professor is going to."

"He'll have a jolly long walk then, that's all I can say to that. And what are we going to do? Sit here and wait till he comes back with some Green Hellebore and then steal it from him?"

"No, we're going too."

"I'm jolly sure we're not going to do anything of the sort. It's absolutely miles and miles. Have you gone crazy?"

"Not in the least. It isn't all that far. I measured it and it's only about six miles to the wood."

"Yes, but we'd have to come all the way back again, and that would make twelve."

"Well, what about it? You know quite well that I've often walked more than twelve miles, with lots of it uphill too."

"Well, you're not going to walk along the Dyke, not all the way to the far end of it anyway. I absolutely forbid you."

"Let's have some breakfast."

"It's no good trying to change the subject."

For answer Sally tipped up the haversack and out of it there tumbled quite a supply of provisions, including bread, butter and two eggs.

"I suppose we're going to eat raw eggs to strengthen us for our expedition across the Sahara desert."

"Don't be silly. They're hard-boiled."

So they were too. Sitting in the dinghy, half hidden among the reeds, they ate their breakfast of bread and butter and hard-boiled eggs washed down with cold water.

"Come on," she said, when they had both finished. "Let's just push the dinghy a little farther among the reeds and then we can be off."

"Where to?"

"The wood of course, you gowk, where do you think?"

"You're not still thinking you're going to walk all that way?"

"Of course I am."

"Did you bring the flower book with you?" Sandy asked as an idea suddenly entered his head.

"Yes, it's under the thwart here. What do you want it for?"

"Just to look up something," he answered, as he turned the pages over till he found the piece about the Hellebores.

"There you are. I knew it wasn't going to be any good. It says here that Green Hellebore flowers from March to May. It'll be over now, so what's the good?"

Sally looked so downcast for a moment that Sandy almost wished his idea had not worked quite so well – but not for long.

"How do we know it needs to be flowering? It's probably the leaves or the stem or perhaps even the seed that you need. You know, like poppy seeds and opium. Anyway, it's only June now and all our things in the garden at home were terribly late this year. I distinctly remember Mummy saying what a late spring it had been."

She was still as determined as ever, but there were times when Sandy could be determined too. He could not exactly use force to stop her, though there was to come a time later that day when he wished that he had.

"All right," he said. "If you're so determined, you'd better get started. It will take a good five hours of walking there and back without much time allowed for rest."

"Good. I knew you'd agree in the end. Come on. Let's get started."

"Goodbye, have a nice walk."

"B-but – you don't mean you're not coming with me?"

"That's just exactly what I do mean. Goodbye. Off with you. I'll look after the dinghy and expect you back here some time this afternoon. You'd better take the haversack with something to eat."

"But you can't let me go off all by myself. You know how cross Daddy will be."

"I'm not frightened of Daddy. If you want to go you can, but I'm not coming."

"But I might get lost."

"I expect you will, but you could take the map and it looks fairly straightforward to me."

"But I might meet a – a – a wolf or a bear or get stolen by gypsies."

"Almost sure to, I should think."

"And – and supposing it thunders?"

"It looks to me rather as if it might. A lot of things could happen before supper-time."

"Oh how I hate you!" Sally suddenly turned on her brother in a furious rage, though he could see she was near to tears at the same time. "I hate you, I hate you and I think you're absolutely beastly to me and I don't care what happens and I'm jolly well going to walk to that wood even if I do have to go alone!"

A real quarrel with Sally was a thing that he had never

had before, and it was certainly the last thing in the world that he wanted after all the fun and excitement of the past few days, but he knew that he must do everything possible to stop her. The distance had very little to do with it, because she was a wonderful walker, and Sandy knew perfectly well that she had managed much longer walks. The walk along the Dyke would be almost flat the whole way and much of it was familiar to them, although they had never been all the way to the far end. She sat there sobbing bitterly, half in anger and half in sheer disappointment.

"Oh all right then," she said sulkily. "I suppose we might as well go back to *Dutchman*, but I'm going for a walk up to the village first."

"That's better," said Sandy, turning towards her at last. "I'll come with you."

"Oh no you won't," she snapped back. "I don't want you and I'd much rather go by myself."

She climbed out of the boat so clumsily that she slipped and put one leg up to her knee in the water. Sandy leant out to help pull her out but she pushed his hand angrily away.

"Let go, will you! I can manage quite well by myself, if only you'd stop interfering. I wouldn't have got wet if you hadn't rocked the boat."

There seemed to be nothing else that Sandy could do, so he turned his back on her and let her go off on her walk up to the village. So all the fun and excitement had come to nothing, and the end of everything was simply to be a bitter quarrel. Sandy wished they had never seen Pout or the Professor or *Fen Tiger*. Feeling very miserable and wondering whether perhaps he had been wrong after all, he began to clear up the remains of their breakfast. He thought that as she would probably be back in a minute or two he might as well turn the dinghy round so that they would be ready to start back to *Dutchman* as soon as she arrived.

Then it was simply a question of waiting, so he waited –

and waited. What a long time she seemed to be taking! Oh well, perhaps it was a good thing. She would have a better chance of getting rid of her temper. But still, it could hardly take more than a couple of minutes up to the village, and there was not a great deal to see when you did get there – just a few old houses and the end of the Dyke. There were not likely to be many people about. What on earth could she be doing all this time?

CHAPTER SIXTEEN

Along the Dyke

Doubts began to creep into Sandy's head, so he tried to busy himself doing this and that, but it was no good. His doubts began to grow, and doubt suddenly became certainty.

He knew quite well that Sally was not coming back for a long time yet. What an idiot he had been not to think of it before! He should never have let her go off by herself like that! But she was gone all the same – and she wasn't coming back either.

Pushing the dinghy higher up into the reeds and hanging the haversack and water-bottle over his shoulders, he set off to follow her. It took him only a moment or two to reach the village green, and as he stopped to look around, a voice hailed him.

"You lost someone?"

"Yes, as a matter of fact I have. I'm looking for my sister. Did you see which way she went?"

"Can't say that I did really. You see, I don't know what your sister looks like."

The man continued on his way, and then looking back over his shoulder he called out, "Has she got black hair?"

"Yes, she has. Have you seen her?"

"I don't know, I tell you. I did see a girl with black hair a little while ago."

"Which way was she going?"

"Looked to me as if she might be going up the Dyke. I did call out to her but I reckon she was in too much of a hurry to take much notice."

"How long ago would that be?"

"Well, let me see now, maybe an hour, or maybe even an hour and a half."

There was obviously no time to be lost now, so with a very quick word of thanks Sandy headed across the open green towards the end of the Dyke where it lay like some gigantic dragon that had come prowling down the hill to drink in the fen, only to have its head cut off by the angry villagers.

An hour – or an hour and a half. That was a very long start on a six-mile walk and if she was moving quickly she might well be getting on towards halfway by now. She would know that he would be certain to follow her eventually and that would make her hurry all the more. He had no hope of getting a sight of her, not yet at least, because that end of the Dyke was all covered with a scrub of thorns and briars that completely obscured the view ahead and made walking difficult as well.

Sandy hurried as best he could, but it was a nightmare walk. On and on he went, longing to get out into the open stretch across the heath, seeming never to get any farther at all, and for ever tripping over long trailing brambles. Pout should have been there to remind him not to be in such a hurry, for he might then have made better speed. What made it so much worse was the realization that Sally would almost certainly be out on the heath by now and that meant that the distance between them would be increasing instead of narrowing.

Stumbling along, as one does in a dream, Sandy caught his foot in a root and fell heavily. Ill luck, or something worse, had made him fall just where, for the first time since he had left the village, the steep side of the Dyke was clear of all growth and there was nothing to catch him as, half-winded by the fall, he rolled over the edge of the slope and went tumbling down to the bottom of the ditch a good twenty feet below.

It was a bad fall and it took him a moment or two to get his breath back, but when he picked himself up no damage seemed to have been done, no broken arm, no sprained ankle, just a slight pain in his knee as he put his right foot to the ground. He brushed the chalky dust from his clothing and scrambled up to the top of the Dyke again. This time he set off with a little more care, beginning at last to understand what Pout meant about not being in such a hurry.

A few moments later he caught a glimpse of the open heath beyond, and there at last he was, on familiar ground. Part of the Dyke had been cut away so as to allow the race-course to pass through it, and it was wonderful to be walking across soft open turf again. He quickly crossed the race-course and climbed once more to the top of the Dyke, hoping that he might get a clear view along it for a couple of miles. There was just a chance that he might even catch a glimpse of Sally.

He had forgotten about the little hut that had been built on top of the Dyke, and now cut short the view. It was true that he could see the Dyke beyond and he thought that he could even see one or two people walking along it, but without binoculars there was no hope of picking Sally out among them. He was still a little sore from his fall and he thought that if he had just two minutes' rest he might perhaps get along all the quicker afterwards, so he sat down on top of the Dyke and had a short drink from the water bottle.

That was the first chance he had had of looking at the sky – and over towards the west he saw the dark clouds piling up and up like some immense and infinitely distant range of mountains. There could be no doubt what that meant.

He got up again and felt another twinge of pain in his right knee as he put his foot to the ground. For maybe a dozen steps it hurt and then it seemed to ease a little and he was able to step out more briskly. Of the rest of his journey over the heath there is little that need be told. It was not very far, not as you measure distance on a map, that is.

The children had walked it in winter with the turf frozen hard and the snow lying in drifts in the deep ditch. They had watched the hares lolloping slowly along in front of their little terrier, who yapped with excitement as he foolishly imagined that he was going to catch one. Many a time they had come to look at the flowers that grew so richly all along the great Dyke, and even now there were orchids almost at his feet. But it had never been like this before. Over to his right the storm-clouds were gathering in seething, towering masses. Somewhere out in front was his sister, alone and running into he knew not what kind of danger. And his knee was beginning to hurt now so that he could no longer walk without a limp.

He struggled on as best he could, compelled every now and again to take a rest as his knee became more and more painful – not that rest brought much relief, because each time he started to walk again the pain seemed worse than it had been before. In the end it seemed best to keep going.

At last he found himself across the heath and standing on the edge of the London road, where he had to wait while a convoy of military lorries drove slowly by. There must have been a block farther along the road because the convoy soon came to a dead stop. He wondered for a moment if he might go up to one of the lorries and ask for help, and he even got as far as taking a step or two towards the nearest of them, when a soldier called out cheerily to ask if he would like a ride to the seaside. He realized then that there was nothing that he could tell them that there would be any hope of their believing. They would see that he had hurt his knee and would probably put him off at the nearest hospital, miles away from where he wanted to be.

There was nothing for it but to find Sally for himself. He must go on, even if he had to crawl the last part of the way. There could not be much more than a mile to go now until he reached the wood, and from his memory of the map the wood itself was only about a mile long. The going was still good for a little way after he had crossed the London road. There was a railway to cross and then another road, and it was then that he began to find himself back among a tangled growth of thorn and briar that scratched him sorely as he made his way through. The sharp pricking and scratching of the thorns did at least make some change from the constant pain in his knee.

The going along the Dyke became more and more difficult and eventually he had to leave the top and make his way down to an overgrown path that ran along beside it. Almost without his noticing it the growth of prickly scrub gave way to trees, small trees at first, then taller ones that climbed up to great heights above his head. Beneath these tall and curiously unfriendly trees there was little undergrowth, but in its place he met great spreading thickets of nettles, tall gangling nettles that reached out and stung him spitefully as he made his way along.

This was an evil place beyond any doubt. There was a sour and bitter smell in the air. Here and there dead or dying trees, some half swathed in ivy, leant for support against taller neighbours that had struggled up to draw strength from the fresh air high above. The light – cold, green and half-starved – seemed to play tricks with his eyes so that he lost all sense of distance, and gradually it took on a darker shade as he limped painfully along, looking fearfully about him this way and that.

A moment later a rumble of thunder told him how fast the storm-clouds had been moving. All was still down below where he walked, but he was aware of a distant roaring, almost as of waves breaking on a rocky shore. He fancied himself to be standing on a green sea-bed beneath the giants of an ocean forest, whose heads high above swirled and tossed in a wild frenzy as they were caught in the full blast of the storm.

He was quickly drenched as the torrents of rain broke through the thin covering of leaves. Exhausted, soaked to the skin and in great pain from his knee, he began to feel that he was beaten. He tried calling, but call as he would, he could not even hear the sound of his own voice above the increasing din that roared around him as though he had strayed into the midst of some infernal battlefield. The lightning seemed to be continuous, the thunder unceasing. Crouching for shelter beneath a fallen trunk, he was half blinded by a sudden brilliant flash that split a great tree from top to bottom barely fifty yards from him. It stood for a moment, swayed and then crashed to the ground with a cruel splintering noise that stood out from the roar of the thunder.

In utter terror he leapt to his feet and began running and stumbling towards it, the pain in his knee forgotten. Surely another sound had risen above that din, a voice calling out for help? Four times he stumbled headlong in the rain-drenched nettles before he reached the fallen tree. He looked all around. He called and called again, but there was no sign of her – save for the map, soaked with the rain and pierced through by a blackened splinter of wood where the lightning had struck.

CHAPTER SEVENTEEN

Terror in the Wood

For a moment Sandy stood there unable to move, knowing now what people meant when they spoke of being petrified with fright. His dripping clothes clung to him and the rain streamed down his face and neck. He would have called out for help, but his mouth and tongue were dry and he could not have made any sound to carry above the noise that still deafened him, even if there had been anyone there to hear. Scarcely knowing why, but feeling only that he must do something, however useless it might be, he knelt down to look at the map, its canvas limp and mud-stained, with a hope which he scarcely dared to express even to himself – that he might perhaps have been mistaken. He knew the hope was a vain one even before he looked more closely at his find.

It was their own map, the one that Sally and he had been looking at only a few hours before. There could be no question about that. There ran the straight line of the Dyke.

There was the head of the lode where the little dinghy would be lying in the reeds, probably awash with the rain now. And there, a little farther along, was Pout Hall Fen where *Dutchman* would be, with Mummy and Daddy perhaps wondering if they had been able to find shelter. How much water had leaked through on to Sally's bunk, he wondered. They would be expecting them back before very long and Mummy would be sure to have got a good supper ready for them – a *Dutchman* special, perhaps.

A sudden, vicious crack of thunder brought him out of his daydream. It was no good kneeling down there in the mud. He must try to think. Had Sally been standing there when the lightning struck? It looked very much as if she must have been. Was he absolutely sure that it was her voice that he had heard crying out? He had certainly thought it was at the time, but could he have been quite sure amid all that din? Of course he was sure – no good clinging to that hope. But where was she then? If she had – had been – surely even then she could not have simply disappeared without any trace?

Sandy knew well enough how dangerous it was to stand beneath trees in a heavy thunderstorm, and even if he had not known before, what he had seen only a few moments ago would have taught him his lesson; but he cared nothing for his own safety just now. Perhaps if he looked carefully he might find some other trace of her that would tell him something. The map was securely pinned to the ground where the splinter of the stricken tree had pierced it, but the wood had gone through near to one corner and he could still lift up most of it to see what was underneath.

Surely there was something lying there, in that little circle of bare ground. He stretched out a hand to pick it up and found himself holding Sally's penknife, its single blade lying open. He knew it well enough. He had seen it many a time before and had often sharpened the blade for her. What had she been doing with it? He looked again at the place where it had lain, a little puzzled by something about its appearance. Protected by the map, it was still fairly dry – and then he suddenly realized what it was that was puzzling him.

Everywhere else in that part of the wood either there were nettles growing in great spreading patches or else the ground was thickly covered with little seedlings, self-sown from the trees above. Why this little circle of bare earth just here? He looked at it again and saw what he had missed before – the root of a plant cut clean through, and, to make him sure beyond all doubt, he found near by a leaf that he recognized at once as coming from the plant they had seen in the Professor's big book.

So she had found the Green Hellebore after all. It must have been growing just there, its foliage spread over that little circle. The excitement of his discoveries had made him forget for a moment his own wretchedness, but when he stood up again and put Sally's knife in one of his pockets, he all but fell as he put his weight on his injured knee, and he had to lean heavily against the fallen tree to support himself.

There seemed to be no lessening of the fury of the storm. High above, the wind still raged among the tree-tops. The rain poured down with such violence that even the nettles, for all the protection given by the foliage of the trees, were borne down by the weight of its attack, and Sandy's head was battered by the constant crashing of the thunder.

Which way had she gone? Which way? Which way? That idiotic Professor Candlewick, why was he not here? Where was he? Why had the Professor not found his sister and saved her from all this horror? It was all the Professor's fault. But perhaps he had better go on a little farther. The tree had fallen away from him, and maybe she had seen it coming and run off in an attempt to escape. She might have fallen and be lying somewhere not very far away. Using his own knife, he cut off a small branch to use as a stick because he found that he could scarcely put his right foot to the ground at all now.

Hobbling painfully, he struggled a little farther through the wood, but he did not get very far. That tall tree laid low by the lightning must have left something of a gap into which the wind could tear with even greater violence. A sense of new and sudden danger made him turn his head to look back over his shoulder, where, to his horror, the noise of its fall deadened by the storm, he saw another tree come crashing down upon the very place where he stood. With one last effort he tried to jump away to one side, but his foot could not grip on the slippery earth and he fell.

He must have lain there many hours. Perhaps he had been struck on the head by a branch and knocked unconscious, though he was not aware of any pain. Perhaps he had not been hit on the head after all, but had simply fallen asleep where he lay, worn out by exhaustion and fright. When he opened his eyes and looked around he saw that the main trunk of the tree was being held a foot or two above him, supported by one of its branches which had been forced deep into the ground a little way to one side. The storm had passed, the wind had died and all around lay a deep silence.

An odd quality in the light puzzled him until, looking out from beneath the tree-trunk which formed a roof over his head, he saw the moon, a little past the full now, shining down through the gap with a clear and friendly light. He stretched out at full length on his back and lay there gazing up at it. Occasionally a thin wisp of cloud hurried across its face and away to the edge of the clearing a single star shone faintly.

How wonderfully peaceful it was, and so comfortable too, almost as if he was safely at home in his bed. So it was all over. Whether he had won or lost was not of the smallest importance to him or to anybody else either. What was it that he had been trying to do, anyway? Never mind. It was finished now. Forget about it. Forget about everything and just lie there for ever and ever, happy and comfortable, watching that glorious moon – a friendly moon too – perhaps – perhaps – perhaps even a talking moon – well, why not try?

"Hallo, Moon," he said. It was odd how clear his voice sounded, almost as if it were not himself but somebody else speaking.

"Hallo, Moon," he said again. "I know a poem about you. Would you like to hear it?"

He paused to listen for a moment. And then went on.

"This is how it goes –

> Slowly, silently, now the moon
> Walks the night in her silver shoon.

Rather nice, isn't it? Do you like it? Shall I go on?

> This way and that she peers, and sees
> Perry merry dixi, dominees."

He paused again, a little puzzled – and then continued.

"Not right? No, I thought not, somehow. Sally would know, though. You just ask her next time you see her. You know, Moon, people are really very silly about your face – those marks on it, I mean. They say they're mountains – the Mountains of the Moon. Stupids! How could they possibly know?

"But I know, don't I, Moon? Especially that one in the middle – that was the hole where the tail came through, wasn't it? Dear, kind Moon. Did you like having a tail or did it get blown about in the wind? I wonder if you wagged it when you were pleased, like a cat, or whether you waved it when you were angry, like a dog. Or was it the other way round? What a pity you lost it! You really ought to be more careful, you know. But never mind, I won't be cross this time. Besides, don't tell anyone, but I know where I could get you another one. It belongs to a man whose coat was red and whose breeches were blue.

"Don't go, Moon. No, please don't go. You say it's time to start getting ready to set? I'm sure it can't be time yet. Stay just a little longer while I listen to you waxing and waning. But of course you can't be doing both at the same time, can you? How stupid of me. Just let me shut my eyes and listen and then I'll tell you which it is. I know – you're waning, aren't you? You always sound a little sad when you're waning. Oh, but you've gone! You slipped round the corner when I had my eyes shut. Come back, come back, Moon! You wouldn't surely leave me all alone, would you? It's dark down here without you and I was so happy talking to you. Never mind, I'll have a little sleep and then perhaps you'll come back again.

"Sh! What was that? Something moving down there in the wood. There it is again. Over there, behind that tree. It's coming this way. I know. It's stupid old Corny Candlewick, but he won't catch me. He doesn't know how well I can fly now – much better than he can. I bet he can hardly get off the ground at all. It's terribly easy really, much easier than swimming. Off we go, in and out among the trees, not too high to begin with. Whoosh! That was lovely, wasn't it!

"What are all those things down on the ground there? They weren't there before – all those little eyes – like shiny black beads – and they're all looking at me. Hedgehogs! That's what they are. Hundreds and hundreds of them and all looking up at me. But I'm all right. Hedgehogs can't fly – or can they? That one down there looks as if he might be going to try – and he is too, and there's another – and another. They're all flying. And they're coming after me. Up higher – that's where I must be – much, much higher – right up above the tree-tops. Here I am again, Moon. So you haven't set after all. Stupid hedgehogs, they thought they could catch me, but they can't fly up here, can they?

"Sh! What's that noise? The hedgehogs, they're coming out through the tops of the trees – hundreds and hundreds and hundreds of them – and all with shining black eyes looking straight at me! They're chasing me! Up, up, up, I must get up, higher and higher, then they won't catch me. I'm coming, Moon! I won't be long now and you will keep me safe, won't you? They're catching me up. I can't get any higher – I'm going to fall. Help, help, Moon! Let down your tail so that I can catch it – it's no good. I'm falling. Help! Catch me! Save me! ... "

"Now then, son, take it easy. Just try this."

Sandy felt a strong arm holding him up as something was put to his lips – the water-bottle, of course. How clever of him to remember it. That's what he needed more than anything – just a good long pull at the water-bottle.

"Steady on now, steady on!"

Must be the moon. What a kind and gentle voice she had, he thought, as the strong arm lowered him down again. Yes, it must be the moon. There it was shining brightly above his head. So he had managed to get right up after all. That must be a record flight. No wonder he was feeling tired. The moon went out quite suddenly. How kind of her to go out just when he wanted to go off to sleep again.

They told him afterwards that he slept for a whole day and a night and half the next day. Certainly when next Sandy opened his eyes, the sun was shining brightly through an open window on to the bed on which he lay. He looked at the ceiling, at the walls, at the windows, but all was strange and unfamiliar. It was certainly not his own bedroom at home. He tried to sit up but found that he could not do so. All he could manage was to raise his head a little, and just as he was wondering what to do he heard voices as the door opened.

"Well, nurse, how's the patient this morning?"

"He was still asleep last time I looked. But I do believe he's awake now, at long last."

Two people, a man and a nurse, went over to his bed.

"Well, well, that's better, and how are you feeling?"

"All right, thank you, but I don't seem able to move about very much. What's happened and where am I?"

"Safe and sound in hospital with nothing more to worry about."

"But – but what — "

"All right now, take it easy. I said you've nothing at all to worry about and I meant what I said. What about your sister? That's it, isn't it?"

Sandy's throat had suddenly gone dry as memory came flooding back and try as he would he could not utter a sound, so he nodded his head.

"Just for a second, Nurse, and no longer."

"Doctor says you can come in, but only for a second."

The door opened wider, and round it came Sally's face.

"All right, you needn't be frightened," said the nurse. "He doesn't bite, so you can come right in and let him see that lovely sling of yours. There you are. She's quite all right. Nothing but a badly sprained wrist."

"But – but that tree – and – and the lightning ... "

"Not now," said nurse firmly. "You'll hear all about everything at the proper time. Come along, Sally, now. Doctor's orders."

They kept Sandy in hospital for nearly a week longer, and very miserable he was for much of it. His right leg was all cased in plaster so that he could not bend it and his back and shoulders were full of aches and pains. Try as he would, he could not get himself into a comfortable position. More than once the nightmare storm came back to him in his dreams, but there came one morning, after he had slept soundly all night, when he woke to find that all his aches had completely left him and he knew he was better. It was all he could do not to jump out of bed and run across to look out of the window, but of course his plaster leg would never have let him. The next day he was allowed to go home. It was soon after breakfast that nurse came in to tell him, and to tell him also that he had a visitor, although she had no business to be there at that hour.

"Ooh, you are lucky!" he heard Sally's voice saying before she was even into the room. "They never put any plaster on my wrist and I'm sure it was just as bad as your silly old knee. And now they're going to bring you home in an ambulance. I heard someone telling nurse it would be ready in half an hour."

"Come on now, young miss. Off with you. You've no business to be in here at this time of day. I'll have to give this brother of yours a bit of help, though I can't think what he needs an ambulance for. He ought to go home on his bicycle, that's what I say."

"I say, Nurse ... "

"Well, what is it?"

"Could she come in the ambulance with me, do you think?"

"Certainly not. I never heard such an idea in all my life. What next!"

A few moments later two men came into Sandy's room with a stretcher on to which he was lifted, and then they carried him off.

"Poor old chap," one of them said to the other as they went.

"Never walk again, they say."

"Had to take the knee right out."

"Give him a cork one instead."

"Bet it'll creak when it bends."

"If it ever does bend."

They spoke in such solemn voices that for a moment Sandy was completely taken in, but as they reached the ambulance the one in front turned and gave him a broad wink, and he knew they were only joking. What a wonderful ambulance it was too, when he saw it. Its bright blue paint was spotlessly clean, its chromium shone in the sun and up on the roof above the driver's seat the bell sparkled and gleamed. A moment later they were off. What a pity that it was not possible to be driven along and at the same time to be outside in the road, watching it go by and knowing that it was you inside all the time. Sandy was just thinking what a shame it was that they would not let Sally come in too, when a panel of glass between his part and the driver's seat slid back – and through it came Sally's face.

"There, that gave you a surprise, didn't it?"

"How on earth did you get there?"

"Oh, I just manage things."

It was not very far to go and they had soon turned into the road where they lived. Suddenly over Sandy's head there came a tremendous clanging of the bell.

"Hey, miss, you mustn't do that."

But the bell went on ringing, and, with passers-by turning to watch them go, they swept up to their front door in splendid style.

CHAPTER EIGHTEEN

A Visitor for Tea

There were endless questions Sandy wanted to ask. What had happened to Sally? How had she got home? How had he got out of the wood? And what about the boats? And above all – what about Pout ... and Cerberus? But it was not till after three o'clock in the afternoon that Sandy was allowed to hobble out into the garden and sit on the swing seat.

The garden table was already set for tea and he wondered idly why there were five cups and plates on it. No doubt Mummy had made a mistake. She was sitting there knitting. Sally was sprawling on the grass and Daddy was reading a newspaper.

"Is nobody ever going to tell me what happened?" asked Sandy plaintively.

"Perhaps you had better begin by asking your sister," his father replied.

"Well, what did happen?"

"Well, nothing very much really," Sally answered, sitting up and clasping her knees with her arms. "Though I'm still not quite sure. I've a sort of feeling that there's something missing, only I don't know what it is. It's a bit like a jigsaw with some of the edge missing, or maybe it's one of the middle bits."

"Did you mean just to walk up to the village and back when you left me that morning?"

"I don't quite know what I meant, honestly I don't. When I got up to the village, there didn't seem to be anyone about at all, though I did see a man coming out of one of the houses. Something made me walk up to the end of the Dyke and once I'd begun to walk along it – well, somehow I just couldn't stop. I knew quite well I was doing wrong, but it was no good at all trying to do anything about it. I just had to go on walking, though I don't seem able to remember anything about the walk, whether there were any other people about or anything like that. I've no idea how long I walked for, but in the end I found myself in the wood. Ugh! What a horrid place it was too!"

"So you found that, did you?"

"Yes, beastly. There wasn't anybody there, at least not that I could see, but it was full of all sorts of things that I couldn't see, and they kept looking at me."

"Hedgehogs."

"What about hedgehogs?"

"Oh, nothing. They're nice things really. It doesn't matter now. What happened next?"

"Well, after I'd gone about halfway through, I suddenly had a feeling that I'd gone as far as I had to go. It was as if something had been pulling me along on a string and then had stopped, quite suddenly. I found I was standing by the trunk of a fallen tree, so I sat down on it to rest. I don't think I'd stopped once all the way till then and I know I'd been walking pretty fast. I looked down, and there it was, growing just at my feet."

"The Green Hellebore?"

"Yes, I recognized it at once. Horrid taste it had too."

"You don't mean to say you tried eating it?"

"No, I didn't exactly eat it, but it had rather a tough stalk and when I was cutting it my knife slipped and cut my finger. I suppose some of the juice must have got out of the stalk on to my finger, because when I sucked the cut it tasted absolutely beastly."

"What did you do next? And by the way, here's your knife. I found it lying there."

"Well, I thought it might be a good idea to wrap the Hellebore up in something to keep it from getting damaged, but I hadn't anything to wrap it in, except the map. So I spread the map out, pushing one corner of it under a little branch that was sticking out from the fallen trunk to hold it flat. You know the way maps curl up when you don't want them to."

"Are you sure that's what you did?" Sandy asked, sitting bolt upright.

"Yes, why?"

"Because you can't possibly have done! I saw that tree fall."

"It must have been some other tree."

"I tell you it wasn't. It can't have been. I wasn't fifty yards away when it was struck by lightning and split right down. It was in the middle of the storm and I was sheltering under another fallen trunk close by. I saw it all as plainly as anything."

"But how do you know it couldn't have been another tree?"

"Because that was when I heard you call out for help. I ran to the tree as quickly as I could and there I found the map with a splinter of the tree holding it down to the ground.

The wood was all blackened and there was a brown mark across the map as if it had been singed. Besides, I found your knife lying underneath it. And I found the stem of the Hellebore where you had cut through it."

There was a sudden stillness in the garden.

"You must be wrong," said Sally quietly. "I never called. You see, I'd left the wood hours before the storm came."

"And I'm absolutely sure I'm right," Sandy answered. "I just don't understand it."

"There's lots of things people don't understand, son. Just let your sister go on."

"Well, for some reason or other, I just forgot all about my idea of wrapping up the plant in the map. I think it was a rabbit that caught my eye and I watched it go hopping away through the wood. Then I picked up the plant and started walking back. I was pretty sure that you would follow me in the end and I expected to meet you on the way back somewhere. But in fact I don't remember meeting anyone much, except some soldiers who offered me a lift to the seaside when I got to the big road."

"What's the matter, son? Knee hurting?"

"No, it's not that. It's just – well, it sounds impossible, but we must have crossed that road in opposite directions at the same time. They offered me a lift to the seaside too! I expect it was the lorries that hid us from one another. Did you get back to the dinghy then?"

"No, I didn't. I walked back across the heath keeping a good look-out for you, but when I'd got most of the way across without seeing you I thought it would be best not to go into that prickly bit in case we should pass each other without knowing it. So I went down off the Dyke on to the grass and sat down for a bit of a rest. I suppose I must have gone to sleep because the next thing I knew was that it was thundering and pouring with rain. I thought I'd better find some shelter as soon as I could, but I must have taken a wrong turning."

"Weren't you terrified by the storm?"

"Well, as a matter of fact it was a bit frightening, but I think it must have been much worse down at the far end of the Dyke by that horrid wood. It was terribly black over there and the lightning seemed to be flashing all the time. I was jolly glad I wasn't there. It must have been dreadful."

"It was. There's no need to tell me that."

"Anyway I kept walking and eventually I came to a road. I thought it would probably bring me to some place where I could shelter and get dried a bit, and when I got over the top of a hill I saw those two church towers. You know, the two that stand side by side in the same churchyard. I remembered that one of the churches was in ruins and wasn't supposed to be safe but I wasn't sure which one it was. I left the road, went across a field and came to a gate that led through into the churchyard. I suppose I must have chosen the wrong church, but it was pretty dark with all those clouds about. I pushed a door open, tripped over something and fell headlong. And that was that."

"Sally dear, just run along and see if there's anyone there, will you? I thought I heard the bell."

"Oh for goodness' sake don't let anyone be coming to tea! Not today of all days! I haven't heard half of it yet. Oh no!! Not him, please not him of all people!!!"

Sandy's heart sank within him as he looked out over the back of the swing seat to see Sally coming back across the lawn with – Professor Candlewick.

"He's a frightful old gasbag and he'll never go, I'm sure. What's he want here anyway? For goodness' sake don't ask him to stay to tea."

"Ah-ha! So there he is! The gallant and ever youthful Sir Alexander, taking his ease on the lawns of his ancient family seat. Charming! Quite charming! First we meet beneath the great lantern-tower whose splendour, if I remember rightly, made you doubt the very possibility of what you beheld with your own eyes. On that occasion you sought to run away from me. Next we meet again upon a little hilltop whose whereabouts perhaps ought not to be revealed to your aged father and mother – to whom I offer my humble greetings – and on that occasion, if memory fails me not, I ran away from you.

"Ah-ha! I perceive that you smile, doubtless recalling the somewhat undignified method of my hasty departure. And now, dear b – that is, aged sir – if I mistake me not, you would gladly run away from me. Is it not so? But there I have you! Your knee, your poor knee, I fear it keeps you a prisoner within the grounds of your own castle. Next time we shall scarcely know whose turn it is to run away – or, shall we say, whose to chase? The teapot! Ah, the teapot. How delicious! What could possibly be nicer? No, no, don't move, I beg you. I shall find myself a chair."

And off he went waddling away across the lawn to get himself a chair. Of all the cheek! Inviting himself to tea like that!

"Bother this beastly knee of mine. If it wasn't for that I should get up and run away before he gets back. And now I'll have to wait for absolutely ages before I know how Sally got out of the church, and I still don't know how I got out of the wood."

"Why don't you try asking Professor Candlewick?" said his father in a voice so soft that Sandy doubted whether he could have heard rightly what he said.

"I said why don't you try asking the Professor?" he repeated as the Professor himself came back with his chair and beamed at Sandy through his gold-rimmed glasses. "After all, he did save your life – and Sally's."

Having learnt what it meant to be petrified with fright, Sandy now understood what it was to be struck dumb with amazement, and so evidently did Sally. They looked at one another, then at the Professor, who was helping himself to a large cream bun, and then at their father, neither of them knowing what to say.

"I always think," said the Professor, as he munched away, "that cream buns should come at the beginning. Take what you can while you can get it and leave the bread and butter till another day.

"Your father is an excellent man," he continued, after he had finished his cream bun and was wiping his fingers on an enormous red handkerchief, "but I fear he exaggerates. For all his seven hundred years, he has not yet learnt that it is best to keep to the literal truth – so much more exciting."

"But I don't understand." It was Sally who was the first of them to find words again. "We chased you along the river and up the lode, but we never saw any sign of you after *Fen Tiger* had left her moorings in the lode. I don't believe it. I think Daddy's just pulling our legs."

"In that case," the Professor began, and then suddenly went off into that peculiar whiffling and chuffling noise that he made when he laughed, "in that case (whiffle), my dear (chuffle), he must have pulled your brother's leg (whiffle chuffle) much too hard (chuffle whiffle chuffle)!"

It was some minutes before he recovered, but he certainly had them all laughing, not so much at his own joke about Sandy's knee as at his own huge enjoyment of it. Sandy looked at him again and thought that behind those huge moon-like lenses in their shining gold frames, he could see a twinkle that he had not noticed before.

"Is it really true," he asked, "what Daddy says about you saving our lives?"

"Dear boy, I am, as you rightly observed a moment or two ago, a frightful old gasbag – no, no, not a word, I beg of you – my hearing is uncommonly sharp for my years, and you are undoubtedly right. Gasbag is the perfect description – "

(and there was just the beginning of another chuffle but it never came to anything) " – but I am a lonely gasbag. I live alone in my crooked house with my books and Elegabalus – my ginger cat, you know. His tail makes an excellent bookmarker when he's asleep. So when I come out I like to talk."

"But what made you talk to us?" Sally asked, as he paused to help himself to another cream bun. They had to wait patiently for his answer while he ate it.

"Living alone and reading my books, I learn many things, some beautiful, some ugly, some frightening and some dangerous. When I go walking about in my lovely cathedral – I look upon it as all my very own, you know – and I find a boy talking aloud to himself about his inability to believe that something is true, I begin to wonder whether all is well with that boy. After all, I think, most people will believe anything. And when, a little later on, as I am walking in the old monastic vineyard, I hear that boy's sister singing a tune to words that she certainly never learnt at school, I begin to wonder a little more and I tell myself to beware of the arrow that flieth by day and the pestilence that walketh in darkness."

"Then – then you didn't really believe that we were six hundred years old?"

"Who knows what I believe? And who, for that matter, knows how old you are?"

"But the soup ... "

"Ah yes! The soup – not very nice to be sure, I must admit that. Terrible indigestion it gave me. No doubt you observed how it doubled me up as I went rolling down the hill."

"But I thought ... "

"Yes my dear, I know what you thought. It was a risk which I could venture to take with myself, knowing as I did that we Candlewicks have always been of strong constitution, but it was not a risk that I could allow you to take."

"You mean that he was going to give the soup to us?" Sandy asked, as he began to have some glimmering of an understanding of what it was all about.

"I mean precisely that. It might not have worked, of course, but I could not be sure."

"But that great big flower book you had, and letting off that huge gun in *Fen Tiger* ... "

"Yes, I expect you found it a little curious, but that was indeed what you were meant to find. Consider my problem. How could I be sure of keeping in touch with you? Then I remembered the Candlewick motto."

"What's that?" they both asked at the same time.

" 'Never do anything yourself if you can persuade anyone else to do it for you!' "

"But that's rule five," said Sally.

"I know it is, my dear. We Candlewicks have lived in the Fens for a long time too. It is not for me to chase them, I thought, let them chase me instead, but I must make as sure as I can that they do not lose me, for if that were to happen then I would have lost them."

"So that was why you fired the gun and dressed up in those extraordinary clothes – to attract our attention."

"Exactly. I hoped that your father would know about the man whose coat was red and whose breeches were blue, and I was not disappointed. I fear I did give your dear mother rather a shock earlier in the day. That was one of my two mistakes. I thought that you and your excellent brother were away walking along the floodbank and that I might have some chance of discussing my plans with your worthy parents, but unfortunately I had to wait for my opportunity till later in the evening."

"Yes, I found your note."

"My note, do you mean?" Sandy asked, turning towards his father.

"No, son. At least, we did find your note and it was

very helpful, but this was a rather longer note from the Professor."

"What was your second mistake?" Sally asked.

"I forgot my Latin."

"How do you mean you forgot your Latin?"

"*Divide et impera.*"

"What's that mean?"

"Divide and rule. I thought that you would be sure to keep together, but alas, the enemy divided you against one another and I was very nearly beaten as a result. Imagine my horror when the Lady Sarah came to the wood alone."

"How did you know I was going to the wood?"

"Because I was nearer than you thought when you discussed your plans, before you had the argument that divided you. You will recall that you never saw me after I had done my little piece of sentry-go beside my devil-scarer.

"Rather clever, that hedgehog, don't you think? I thought the peewits would probably attack it. I saw you pick the Hellebore and I followed you back, but then came the brave Sir Alexander.

"No, no, dear boy, I assure you that I am not laughing at you. You may not have known just how great were the perils that faced you, but you stuck gallantly to it. What was I to do? Which to follow? The wood – that was the dangerous place. Let the raven-haired Lady Sarah get safely out on the open heath, I thought, and no great harm could befall her there.

"She had no fear, you see, and that was her strongest defence. So I followed her back along the Dyke until she decided to leave it and take a rest. Then I left her. It was a risk, I knew that, but it had to be taken. Back I went to the wood as fast as my short legs would carry me, hoping that I might not be too late. When I first caught sight of you lying there I thought that I was indeed too late."

"And then what?"

"Why, there's little more to tell. I was able to carry you farther on through the wood and there I found your father and mother waiting with the ambulance."

"Yes, we had a job getting it there, I can tell you, and keeping it until you turned up. The driver thought we were both quite mad."

"But how on earth did you know that you would be needed there?"

"Thanks to the far-sighted Professor Candlewick, who had carefully informed us of his plan of battle in a note which he pushed through the port-hole on to my bunk. Though I must admit that it gave us a very nasty shock when we found that Sally wasn't with you. However, he assured us that all would be well and as you were obviously in a bad way we thought we had better get you straight off to hospital as quickly as we could."

"What about Sally? How did she get back?"

"By taxi," replied the Professor.

"By taxi? What on earth do you mean?"

"Well, she has already told you how she found her way to the two churches."

"Did you go there too?"

"I did."

"But how did you know you would find her there?"

"I didn't know, but I guessed. You see, I knew why she wanted the Green Hellebore. The problem of that four-footed creature called Cerberus has often puzzled me when I have been sitting alone with my books, but it was out there in the storm that the answer suddenly came to me.

"Have you ever looked carefully at those two church towers? The Normans built one of them at about the same time as they were building their great cathedral. They gave it eight sides – like the great lantern that was built after their cathedral tower fell down. They gave it walls six feet thick, and if you look in one corner of that tower you will find a winding stair, and a little way up that stair you will see some curious slits, rather like prison windows. The other tower is not quite so old, and if you go there and have a look up at it you will see gazing down at you two strange creatures. One of them has a long tongue hanging out and I think he might be a dog, though some might think him a wolf. The other has a sulky, ugly, but strangely powerful face. I have often wondered whose those faces are."

"Cerberus and Pout?" said Sally questioningly. "So that was where they put Cerberus. Up in that old Norman tower."

"That was their real mistake," the Professor went on, as if to himself. "They were so sure they were right. They thought they knew all the answers, but there was always something that worried them at the back of their minds – fate, chance, luck – call it what you will, sometimes good, sometimes bad, but they could never tell which it was going to be, so they tried to catch it, put it in prison and then pretend it wasn't there any more. But it was. And it still is."

"Sally dear," her mother said, "would you like to run up to my room and look on the top of the wardrobe. You'll find a box there wrapped up in brown paper. Bring it down, will you, and be careful with it."

"Whereabouts did you find Sally?" Sandy asked when his sister had gone.

There was a moment's silence and Sandy felt that perhaps he ought not to have asked the question.

"I think you can trust him," his father said eventually.

"Half up the stair of that old Norman tower, lying with one foot wedged in the masonry."

"Do you – do you mean that she nearly fell?"

"Yes, but she must never, never know. Promise me that."

The horror of it all began to come back to Sandy, but just then Sally came skipping across the lawn.

"Do be careful, dear. It's a very precious parcel."

"Sorry, I forgot. I know there was something else I

wanted to ask about. What happened to the boats? They aren't still down there, are they?"

"Oh no, we got them back all right."

"And now, Professor Candlewick," said Mummy, "the aged, but ever youthful Sir Alexander and his almost equally aged, but no less youthful sister, the Lady Sarah, wish to make you a small presentation."

The Professor stood up and bowed deeply, first to Sally and then to Sandy, so deeply that he all but toppled over.

"Your servant, madam, your servant, sir."

Her mother gave Sally the box and she, a little puzzled, but curtsying with the greatest dignity, handed it to the Professor.

He removed the brown paper, opened the box and then, kneeling down on the lawn, proceeded to spread out its contents before him in orderly rows. When he had finished he looked up at the children with a beaming smile all over his face.

"Seventy-four pairs," he said. "Seventy-four pairs. Oh happy, happy Candlewick!"

"And now," he said, after putting away all the spectacles in their cases and then putting the cases in a satchel which hung down his back, "and now it is time for me to be getting back to my books. Elegabalus will be waiting for his milk. I believe he was keeping the place for me in a somewhat unusually heavy book and I fear he may have pins and needles in his tail!"

He bowed deeply to each of them in turn and began to walk away across the lawn.

"But Professor Candlewick," Sally called out. "There's something else. What happened to Cerberus? Did he escape?"

The Professor stopped and turned back towards them.

"The Hellebore had disappeared from the church."

And that was all he said.

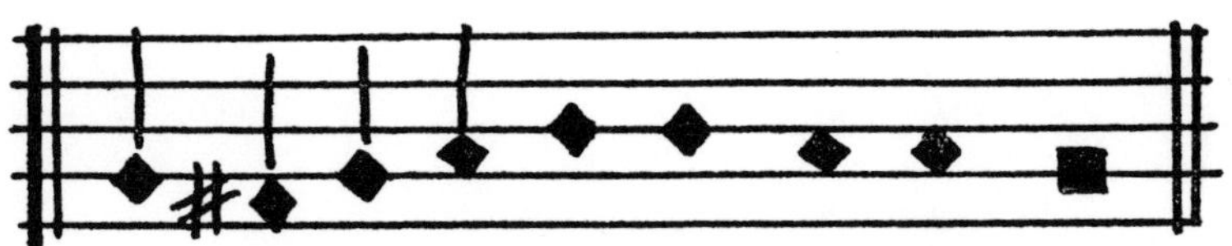

Perry merry dixi, dominee